CLAWS OF ADDICTION

BY
GEOFF DAYBREEZE

This book is dedicated to those that have been lost but are still here in our minds and hearts.
also to my aunt Susan(agnes) who inspired me with the idea for this book and has been a guiding light in all
of this with all that she does
also to those that have helped along the way in terms of giving me critic and honest feedback, thanks guys especially K, L, A & E,
you know who you are

Also......... Enjoy!!!

1

The wind whipped Detective Sarah Mitchell's short brown hair around her face as she stood on the outskirts of the crime scene, her athletic frame tense with determination. In her mid-30s, she had a fire in her eyes that only burned brighter every time someone doubted her abilities.

The salty sea air stung Sarah's nostrils as she stepped onto Clacton-on-Sea's bustling pier. The quaint town, with its rows of colorful beach huts and narrow streets lined with charming shops, seemed an unlikely setting for a gruesome murder. Seagulls screeched overhead as children laughed on the carousel and couples strolled hand-in-hand along the wooden planks. Underneath the facade of gaiety, however, a sinister undercurrent gripped the pier.

"Another day, another gruesome case," muttered Charlie Reynolds, her seasoned partner, as he approached her. His salt-and-pepper hair disheveled from the gusty breeze.

"Let's just hope this one doesn't end up like the others," Sarah replied, her voice strained. She couldn't shake the memory of her last failed investigation, which still haunted her dreams.

"Hey, we'll get through this, kid," Charlie reassured her, clapping a hand on her shoulder. "You're one of the best detectives I've ever worked with."

"Thanks, but it feels like my luck's run out," Sarah admitted, her mind drifting to the dark vice that consumed her nights – gambling. The thrill of the game had hooked her, but the mounting debts and failures chewed away at her soul. She knew she needed to overcome her addiction if she wanted to save her career, but the compulsion was overpowering.

"Sarah, focus," Charlie said firmly, snapping her back to the present. "We've got a job to do."

"Right," she agreed, steeling herself for the task at hand. As they approached the crime scene, Sarah's thoughts raced. This case was her chance to prove herself – to silence the whispers of doubt that followed her every move. But she also knew the stakes were higher than ever. If she lost control of her addiction during the investigation, it could cost her everything.

"Looks like we found our crime scene," she muttered, striding toward him. Her heart pounded as she fought the urge to place a bet at the nearby arcade games. Gambling was her crutch, but she couldn't afford any distractions now.

"Right, so Richard Evans." Charlie flipped open his notebook. "Local businessman, shady past, lots of enemies."

"Great," Sarah sighed, scanning the area for potential witnesses. "Just what we need."

"Take a look at this," Charlie said, nodding toward the claw grab machine.

Sarah peered inside and gasped. Richard Evans' lifeless eyes stared back at her, his once-pristine suit now soaked with blood. A chill ran down her spine as she realized the full magnitude of their situation.

"Whoever did this wanted to send a message," she whispered, swallowing hard. "We can't let them get away with it."

"Agreed," Charlie said, placing a comforting hand on her shoulder. "But we've got to stay focused, Sarah. You know that, right?"

"I know," she replied, clenching her fists. "I won't let my addiction control me. Not this time."

"Good. Now let's get to work."

"First thing tomorrow, we'll start canvassing the area," Sarah announced, already planning their next steps. "We need to find out who saw or heard anything. We can't afford any more mistakes."

"Agreed," Charlie nodded. "But for now, let's focus on what's in front of us. You ready?"

"More than ever," Sarah replied, her eyes set firmly on the crime scene ahead, knowing that this case could make or break her career. She steeled herself against the demons within, determined not to let them control her destiny. This time, she would emerge victorious – no matter the cost.

•••

The salty sea breeze mixed with the scent of spilled popcorn, as seagulls squawked overhead. The pier hummed with the chatter of tourists and the buzz of amusement rides, but Sarah's eyes were drawn to the macabre centerpiece of this carnival: the claw grab machine, its metallic talons gripping Richard Evans' severed head.

"Jesus Christ," Sarah muttered under her breath, her pulse quickening. She couldn't tear her gaze away from the grisly sight – the victim's lifeless eyes staring back at her, blood dripping down the strands of his short grey hair.

"Never seen anything like it, have you?" Charlie asked, his voice betraying a hint of unease.

"Can't say I have." Sarah's voice was steady, but her clenched fists told a different story. Her determination flared as she carefully observed the crime scene, making mental notes about potential evidence.

"Looks like they wanted to make a statement," Charlie remarked, glancing around at the stunned onlookers.

"Then we need to figure out what that statement is," Sarah replied, stepping forward for a closer look. "And who's behind it."

"Right." Charlie nodded, watching as Sarah snapped on her latex gloves and began examining the scene more closely. "I'll question the operator. See if he noticed anything."

"Good idea," Sarah said, her focus never leaving Richard's dismembered face. She leaned in, searching for any signs of struggle, her mind racing with questions. Who would do this? And why?

As she worked, Sarah felt the familiar itch of her gambling addiction gnawing at the edges of her consciousness. The odds, the stakes – it all called to her like a siren song. But she couldn't afford to lose herself in that darkness now. There was too much at stake.

"Sarah?" Charlie's voice snapped her back to reality. "You okay?"

"Fine," she replied, steeling herself against her demons. "Just focused."

"Good." Charlie gave her a reassuring pat on the back. "We'll get to the bottom of this. Together."

"Damn right we will," Sarah said, her determination unwavering as she continued her meticulous examination of the horrifying scene before her. This was her chance to prove herself – and she wouldn't let anything stand in her way.

•••

"Detective Mitchell, a word, please," Inspector Martin Davis called out, his booming voice echoing across the crowded pier. Sarah looked up from Richard Evans' mutilated body, her heart sinking at the sight of her superior officer approaching with a stern expression etched on his face.

"Sir?" she asked, standing to attention as Davis stopped beside her.

"Reynolds has filled me in on your initial findings," he said, glancing down at the grisly scene before them. "This case could attract a lot of media attention. I expect you to handle it with discretion and professionalism. And I don't need to remind you that this is your chance to prove yourself."

"Understood, sir," Sarah replied, feeling the weight of his expectations like a physical burden. She noticed Charlie watching them from a distance, concern in his eyes.

"Good. I'll be keeping a close eye on your progress." With that, Davis turned on his heel and strode away, leaving Sarah alone with her thoughts.

"Hey," Charlie said, rejoining her side. "Don't let him get to you. We're a team, remember?"

"Of course," Sarah agreed, managing a weak smile. "Thanks, Charlie."

"Anytime." He flashed her a reassuring grin. "Now, let's see if we can make some sense of this mess."

As they resumed their examination of the crime scene, Sarah couldn't help but appreciate the support Charlie provided. He had been her mentor since she joined the force, and over time, they had developed a strong bond. In many ways, he was more than just a partner; he was her rock.

"Found something," Charlie said, pointing to a small scrap of paper wedged beneath the claw machine's base. Carefully, Sarah retrieved the evidence with tweezers, holding it up to inspect it.

"Could be a lead," she mused, her mind already racing with theories. "We should run this through the lab."

"Agreed," Charlie replied, his voice steady and calm. "Let's get it bagged and tagged."

As they worked side by side, Sarah felt a renewed sense of determination coursing through her veins. With Charlie at her side, she could face any challenge, even the suffocating pressure that seemed to follow her around like a shadow.

"Alright, let's wrap things up here for now," Charlie suggested.

"We'll head to the station, start putting together a list of possible suspects."

"Sounds good," Sarah agreed, her gaze lingering on the macabre scene one last time before turning away. Together, they left the pier, the weight of their shared responsibility settling on their shoulders as they embarked on the daunting task of solving Richard Evans' grisly murder.

•••

The flickering neon lights of the pier's amusements cast a garish glow across Sarah's face as she stood outside, trying to shake off the gruesome image that had been seared into her mind. The sound of slot machines chimed in the background, and she felt the familiar itch rising within her — the call of chance that had plagued her for years.

"Hey, you alright?" Charlie asked, concern etching his features as he noticed her fidgeting with the loose change in her pocket.

"Yeah," Sarah forced a smile, swallowing hard. "Just... processing everything." She turned away from the arcade, focusing on the waves crashing against the shore instead, desperate to distance herself from the irresistible pull of the flashing lights and spinning reels.

"Let's talk about the case," Charlie suggested, pulling out a notepad and pen, redirecting their attention to the task at hand. "We need to find some leads. What do we know about Richard Evans?"

"Businessman, shady past," Sarah said, her mind racing through the details they had uncovered so far. "Had some ties to organized crime, but nothing recent."

"Maybe someone from his past caught up with him," Charlie mused, scribbling notes as they spoke. "Or it could be unrelated. Business rivals, personal vendettas – there's no shortage of possibilities."

"Right," Sarah agreed, her thoughts briefly returning to the scrap of paper they'd found earlier. "We should also look into people who frequent the pier. He was killed here, after all."

"Good point," Charlie nodded, adding more notes to his ever-growing list. "And what about that paper we found? We'll get the lab to analyze it, see if it turns up any useful information."

"Definitely," Sarah said, her fingers still itching to slip a coin into one of the nearby slot machines. She clenched her fist, trying to suppress the urge as she focused on the conversation. "We'll need to work fast, though. Davis is breathing down our necks."

"Understood," Charlie replied, his voice firm but reassuring. "We'll follow every lead and turn over every stone. We'll find who did this, Sarah."

"Thanks, Charlie," she said, grateful for his unwavering support.

The temptation beckoned from just a few steps away, but she was determined not to let it compromise her investigation – or her partnership with Charlie.

"Let's get to work," she declared, pocketing the loose change and turning her back on the amusements. Together, they walked away from the pier's dizzying lights and sounds, ready to delve deeper into the mystery that lay before them.

•••

The early morning sun cast long shadows across the worn cobblestone streets of Clacton-on-Sea, as Sarah and Charlie stepped into a small café. The smell of strong coffee and buttered toast filled the air, providing a brief respite from the dark world they were about to delve into. Sarah's fingers twitched involuntarily, the memory of last night's amusements still fresh in her mind. She took a deep breath, looked at Charlie, and nodded.

"Let's do this," she said, determination etched on her face. No matter the risks involved or the temptations that lay in wait, she was going to give this case everything she had.

"First up, we've got the pier attendant who found the body," Charlie said, flipping through his notes. "We'll see if he saw anything useful."

They approached the young man behind the counter, his eyes wide with anxiety. Sarah could practically see the fear radiating off him, but she knew that she needed to remain focused.

"Morning," she greeted, her voice steady. "I'm Detective Mitchell and this is Detective Reynolds. We'd like to ask you a few questions about what you saw last night."

"Uh, sure," the attendant stammered, wiping his hands on his apron. "I didn't really see much, though. I was just closing up when I spotted... well, you know."

"Did you notice anything unusual earlier in the evening?" Charlie asked, his tone gentle but firm.

"Nothing out of the ordinary," the attendant shook his head. "Just the usual mix of tourists and locals, really."

"Any familiar faces hanging around?" Sarah pressed, her mind racing through the possibilities.

"Maybe a couple of regulars," he replied hesitantly. "But nobody that I'd think would be involved in something like this."

"Thank you for your time," Sarah said, her gaze never wavering. "If you remember anything else, don't hesitate to contact us."

As they left the café, Sarah's thoughts turned inward. She knew that this case would test her resolve, both professionally and personally, but she refused to let it break her. She owed it to herself – and to the victim – to see this through.

"Next, we'll check with some of Richard's known associates," Charlie suggested as they walked down the street, dodging a group of giggling children clutching ice cream cones. "He had a few unsavory connections in the criminal underworld, so they might be able to shed some light on who'd want him dead."

"Sounds like a plan," Sarah agreed, steeling herself for the difficult conversations ahead. As they knocked on the door of a grimy flat, she reminded herself that this was her chance to prove that she could overcome her past mistakes and make a difference. And she wasn't about to let that slip away.

•••

The door to the dimly lit pub creaked open, revealing a smoky haze and the sound of laughter and clinking glasses. Sarah's senses were immediately assaulted by the mingling scents of stale beer, sweat, and cigarette smoke. She followed Charlie inside, trying not to let her discomfort show.

"Let's see what Tina Walsh can tell us," Charlie muttered as they approached the bar. A woman with fiery red hair and a knowing smile leaned against the counter, wiping a glass with a cloth. Sarah could feel her eyes scanning them, sizing them up.

"Detectives, what brings you to my humble establishment?" Tina asked in a teasing tone, her green eyes glinting with curiosity.

"Information about Richard Evans," Sarah said bluntly, her gaze fixed on Tina's face. "We're told you know quite a bit about the town's residents."

Tina raised an eyebrow, her smile never wavering. "I might have some gossip here and there. Knowledge is power, after all."

"Any connections between Richard and the criminal underworld?" Charlie probed, his voice stern but not unkind.

"Richie had his fingers in a few pies," Tina admitted, leaning in closer. "Rumors say he was involved in smuggling operations along the coast. Drugs, counterfeit goods, that sort of thing."

Sarah's mind raced, processing this new information and connecting it to the puzzle that was Richard Evans' murder. The web of suspects seemed to grow more tangled by the minute, each thread leading to a new possibility. Her heart pounded in her chest, the thrill of the chase both invigorating and terrifying.

"Did Richard have any enemies around here?" Sarah asked, her voice steady despite her racing thoughts.

"Plenty," Tina replied with a sly grin. "He stepped on a lot of toes over the years. But one name comes to mind – Jimmy 'The Shark' Pearson. He's a local gangster with a penchant for violence and a grudge against Richard."

"Where can we find this Pearson?" Charlie questioned, his expression serious.

"Club Noir," Tina answered, flicking her wrist towards the east end of town. "He's usually there on Friday nights, surrounded by his goons."

"Much obliged, Tina," Sarah said, forcing a smile as she turned to leave.

"Be careful, detectives," Tina called after them, her voice suddenly somber. "Jimmy Pearson isn't someone to be trifled with."

As they exited the pub, Sarah's thoughts swirled with the weight of the information they'd just received. She sensed that every new lead brought them closer to danger, but she couldn't let fear hold her back. Her determination to solve Richard Evans' murder was unwavering, even in the face of her personal demons.

"Looks like we're headed to Club Noir next," Charlie said grimly, his eyes dark with concern. "But be ready for anything, Sarah. We're about to dive into some treacherous waters."

•••

Under a clouded night sky, Sarah and Charlie approached the ominous entrance of Club Noir. The flickering neon sign buzzed above their heads, casting eerie shadows on their faces as they steeled themselves for the confrontation ahead.

"Remember, we're just here to gather information," Charlie whispered, his eyes scanning the dark alleyway that led to the club's entrance. "No heroics."

"Got it," Sarah replied, her jaw set in determination. She couldn't shake the growing sense of unease that gnawed at her insides. Her gambling addiction clawed at the back of her mind, urging her to take one more risk, but she pushed the thoughts away. This wasn't about her demons; it was about justice for Richard Evans.

The heavy door creaked open, revealing the pulsating heart of Club Noir. Thumping bass shook the walls, drowning out any semblance of conversation. Sarah's gaze darted around the dimly lit room, searching for Jimmy 'The Shark' Pearson.

"Over there," Charlie muttered, nodding towards a corner booth where a man with a scarred face and sinister grin held court. His entourage of henchmen loomed nearby, surveying the room with cold, calculating eyes.

"Let's go," Sarah said, taking a deep breath. As they wove through the throng of dancers, her pulse raced with anticipation and fear. She knew they were treading on dangerous ground, but the need to uncover the truth propelled her forward.

"Jimmy Pearson?" Charlie asked loudly, his voice cutting through the music as he reached the booth.

"Who's asking?" Jimmy sneered, his eyes narrowing as he studied the two detectives.

"Detective Reynolds and Detective Mitchell," Sarah replied, flashing her badge. "We have some questions about Richard Evans."

"Never heard of him," Jimmy snorted, his amusement apparent. "Now, if you don't mind, I'm busy."

"Listen," Charlie said, leaning in closer. "We know you had a grudge against Evans. Now he's dead, and we need answers."

"Or what?" Jimmy countered, his voice dripping with menace.

Just then, a gunshot rang out, shattering the cacophony of music and conversation. Sarah instinctively ducked, as screams erupted throughout the club. In the ensuing chaos, she caught sight of a figure slipping out the back door.

"Charlie, someone's getting away!" she shouted, scrambling to her feet. Without waiting for his response, she sprinted after the mysterious figure, her heart pounding in her chest.

As she burst into the dark alleyway, hot on the heels of the fleeing suspect, she realized that the unknown dangers ahead were only just beginning.

2

Detective Sarah Mitchell could feel the weight of Inspector Davis' scrutiny bearing down on her like a leaden cloud. His piercing gaze seemed to bore into her very soul, as if he could read every thought that raced through her mind. The tense atmosphere in the cramped office was almost palpable, thick enough to slice with a knife.

"Sarah, I hope you're ready for this," said the gruff voice of Detective Charles "Charlie" Reynolds, her partner and mentor. He leaned against the doorframe, his salt-and-pepper hair catching the dim light seeping through the blinds. Charlie had seen it all in his years on the force, but there was something about this case that even made him uneasy.

"Of course, Charlie," she replied, trying to mask the tremor in her voice. She clenched her fists tightly, nails digging into her palms - anything to keep the tidal wave of anxiety at bay.

"Good." Charlie stepped forward, placing a reassuring hand on her shoulder. "We've got each other's backs, remember that."

"Thanks, Charlie." Sarah forced a smile, feeling the warmth of their camaraderie cut through the chill of Davis' disapproval. There was something about Charlie's solid presence that bolstered her resolve. He was her rock amidst the swirling storm of doubt and insecurity.

"Alright, let's get to work," Charlie said, patting her shoulder before moving towards the cluttered desk strewn with evidence.

The two detectives dove headfirst into the sea of paperwork, sifting through witness statements and crime scene photos. Each piece of the puzzle only served to deepen the mystery surrounding the case, fueling Sarah's determination to prove her worth in solving it.

"Dammit, there has to be something here," she muttered, her brow furrowed in concentration. She couldn't help but glance over her shoulder, where Inspector Davis' steely gaze still lingered. The pressure was mounting, and Sarah knew she couldn't afford to make any mistakes.

"Take it easy, Sarah," Charlie said softly, noting the tension in her posture. "We'll find what we're looking for. Just breathe." Sarah nodded, taking a deep breath as she tried to center herself. She had to stay focused on the task at hand, not let the specter of failure claw its way into her thoughts.

"Okay, Charlie. Let's do this," she said, steeling herself for the challenge ahead. Together, they continued their search, each new discovery driving them deeper into the darkness that lurked beneath the surface.

And as Sarah felt the strain of Inspector Davis' scrutiny, she also felt the unwavering support of Charlie Reynolds - the one person who always believed in her. With him by her side, there was no mystery too dark, no secret too twisted that they couldn't unravel.

"Come on, partner," Charlie said with a grin, his eyes alight with determination. "Let's show them what we're made of."

●●●

A bead of sweat rolled down Sarah's temple as she and Charlie stood outside Richard Evans' office. The door was imposing, a dark mahogany that seemed to hold secrets within its very grain.

"Alright, Sarah," Charlie said, his voice low and steady. "We need to dig deep into Richard's connections. Find out who he's been dealing with, and why."

"Agreed," she replied, her voice firm, eyes locked on the door. She knew the importance of this case – it could be the key to finally proving her worth as a detective. Her heart raced, fueled by adrenaline and determination.

Charlie produced a set of lock picks from his pocket, quickly working on the door. As the lock clicked open, they exchanged a nod before carefully pushing it ajar.

The office was eerily quiet, dimly lit by the last remnants of daylight seeping through the blinds. Shadows danced across the floor, creating an unsettling atmosphere. Sarah's instincts screamed at her; danger was lurking, hidden beneath the surface of Richard Evans' life.

"Let's start with his desk," Charlie suggested, pulling on a pair of gloves.

"Good idea," Sarah agreed, following suit. They began to sift through the papers, drawers, and personal effects in silence, each aware of the gravity of their task.

"Hey, Sarah," Charlie called out softly, holding up a small notebook. "Looks like we've got some names and numbers here. Might be useful."

"Nice find, partner," she replied, taking the notebook and flipping through it. Her eyes scanned the contents, searching for any indication of the criminal ties they were seeking.

As they continued their search, Sarah couldn't shake the feeling that they were on the verge of uncovering something big. Her mind raced, thoughts darting between potential leads and the ever-present weight of Inspector Davis' expectations.

"Look at this," Charlie said suddenly, holding up a photograph. It depicted Richard Evans shaking hands with a man Sarah recognized as a known criminal figure.

"Good catch," she whispered, her pulse quickening. "We're closing in on it, Charlie."

"Damn right we are," he replied, his eyes gleaming with determination. Together, they continued to explore the depths of Richard's office, each new piece of evidence drawing them closer to the truth that lay hidden in the shadows.

•••

Sarah's eyes caught movement near the office door, and she tensed. A tall man with a sharp jawline and piercing blue eyes entered, his gaze darting around the room as if searching for something. Sarah could see the sweat beading on his forehead, despite the cool temperature in the office.

"Who are you?" Charlie demanded, stepping forward to block the man from advancing further into the room.

"Name's Alan," the man replied, swallowing hard. "I'm Richard's assistant. I heard what happened... I just wanted to see if there was anything I could do to help."

"Help?" Sarah echoed skeptically, noting the nervous tremor in his voice. "How exactly?"

"Look, I've been working with Richard for years," Alan insisted, his hands twisting together anxiously. "I know he had some...

questionable connections. Maybe I can provide some insight or point you in the right direction."

"Or maybe you're more involved than you're letting on," Charlie countered, narrowing his eyes at the man.

"Charlie, let's hear him out," Sarah interjected, her instincts telling her that Alan might be their best lead yet. She watched as Charlie reluctantly backed off, still keeping a wary eye on the newcomer.

"Alright, Alan," Sarah said, folding her arms across her chest. "What can you tell us about Richard's criminal associates?"

Alan hesitated, looking nervously between the two detectives. "There was this one guy...he'd come by the office late at night, always dressed in black. Seemed real shady. I overheard them talking about some deals they were making—big money stuff."

"Did you catch a name?" Charlie asked, his tone gruff but attentive.

"Vince...Vincent something," Alan stammered, wracking his brain for details. "I think he does business at the docks."

"Vincent Russo," Sarah muttered under her breath, recognizing the name from an earlier case. Her heart pounded in her chest as she realized the gravity of the connection. "He's a known mobster."

"Russo, that's it!" Alan exclaimed, relief flooding his face. "I tried to stay out of it, but I knew Richard was getting in too deep with some dangerous people."

"Listen, Alan," Charlie said, his voice firm. "We're going to need you to come with us to give a full statement. And don't even think about leaving town."

"Of course," Alan agreed, his eyes wide. "Whatever I can do to help."

"Sarah, check this out." Charlie held up his phone, displaying a text message from an informant. "Our guy says there's gonna be a meeting tonight between Richard and Russo. We've gotta move on this—now."

"Let's go," Sarah replied, her mind racing with the implications of this new information. The lure of uncovering Richard Evans' criminal connections grew more tantalizing with each passing moment, and she couldn't afford to let this lead slip through her fingers.

•••

The evening air was heavy with the scent of salt and decay as Sarah and Charlie parked their unmarked car at the edge of the docks. Pulsing neon signs from nearby bars reflected off the water, casting a sickly glow on the corroded metal surfaces and slick wooden planks beneath their feet. They watched as Richard Evans emerged from the shadows, his figure hunched and furtive.

"Got him," Charlie whispered, his voice barely audible above the distant hum of traffic.

Sarah nodded, her eyes never leaving the scene unfolding before them. She gripped the steering wheel with white-knuckled intensity, her heart pounding in her chest. This was the break they'd been waiting for, the chance to finally expose Richard's ties to the criminal underworld.

"Remember, we need to stay back and observe," Charlie cautioned, his eyes scanning the area for any sign of Vincent Russo. "We can't afford to spook them."

"I know, I know," Sarah muttered under her breath, her gaze darting between Richard and the entrance to a dimly lit warehouse.

As they waited in silence, tension coiled tightly around Sarah's chest like a python. The familiar itch of her gambling addiction began to gnaw at her, the temptation to place a bet on the outcome of their stakeout becoming almost unbearable. Her palms felt clammy against the leather of the steering wheel.

"Dammit," she cursed quietly, trying to shake off the urge.

"Everything okay?" Charlie asked, concern lacing his words.

"Fine," she lied, forcing herself to focus on the task at hand. "Just watching."

"Good." Charlie offered a small, reassuring smile. "We're gonna nail this guy, Sarah. Trust me."

She took a deep breath, steadying her nerves. The weight of responsibility and her own demons pressed down on her, but she refused to let them win. This case meant everything to her, and she couldn't let it slip away.

"Look!" Charlie hissed, pointing towards the warehouse. "There's Russo."

A tall figure with slicked-back hair appeared from the darkness, the glint of a gold watch catching Sarah's eye as he approached Richard. She held her breath, her hands gripping the binoculars tighter, every muscle in her body tensed.

"Stay cool, Sarah," Charlie reminded her, his own eyes never leaving the pair. "We'll get them. I promise."

"Right," she whispered, swallowing the lump in her throat. "Let's see what they're up to."

As they continued to observe the clandestine meeting, Sarah fought to keep her mind on the job and not on the allure of placing a bet. She knew it was a dangerous game to play, but tonight was about the case – not her demons.

Tonight, justice would prevail.

•••

The tension in the air crackled like electricity, sending shivers down Sarah's spine as she watched Richard and Russo, the criminal figure, engage in a heated exchange. Their voices were muffled by distance, but the anger in their gestures spoke volumes.

"Damn it," Charlie muttered, snapping a photo with his camera. "Wish we could hear what they're saying."

"Body language says enough," Sarah replied, her thoughts racing. What could have ignited such fury between them? The answer might be the key to unraveling Richard's involvement in the criminal underworld.

"Look at that!" Charlie hissed, pointing to Richard's clenched fist.

As if on cue, Richard slammed his hand onto a nearby crate, his face red with rage. Russo narrowed his eyes, stepping closer to Richard, their faces inches apart.

"Whatever they're arguing about, it's big," Charlie whispered, eyes wide. "Real big."

"Could be our break," Sarah agreed, her heart pounding. Was this the moment that would finally expose Richard's secrets?

Then, as suddenly as it had started, the argument ended. Richard stormed off, leaving Russo fuming in his wake. As they disappeared into the shadows, Sarah and Charlie exchanged glances.

"Looks like we've got our work cut out for us," Charlie said, rubbing his chin thoughtfully. "We need a way in. A lead that'll bring us closer to their world."

"Agreed," Sarah said, wracking her brain for any possible connections. "But where do we start?"

"Wait," Charlie's eyes lit up. "I've heard rumors about a bar called The Rusty Anchor. Supposedly, it's a hotspot for the criminal underworld."

"Perfect," Sarah nodded, determination burning in her eyes. "Let's check it out."

As they prepared to leave their stakeout location, Sarah couldn't shake the image of Richard's anger, his face twisted in fury. She had seen many criminals in her career, but something about this moment seemed different. It was personal.

"Whatever you're involved in, Richard," she whispered to herself, "we're going to find out."

•••

The Rusty Anchor's sign flickered above the entrance, casting a dim glow on the wet pavement. Sarah and Charlie stepped inside, the scent of stale beer and cigarette smoke hitting them immediately. The low hum of conversation filled the air as they scanned the room for potential leads.

"Let's start with the bartender," Charlie suggested, nodding towards the woman behind the counter. Her fiery red hair stood out like a beacon in the dimly lit bar.

"Good idea," Sarah agreed, her eyes narrowing as she studied the woman. Tina Walsh was known for her sharp tongue and even sharper ears. If anyone knew something about Richard Evans, it would be her.

"Evening, Tina," Charlie greeted as they approached the counter. "We're looking for some information."

"Detectives," Tina acknowledged, her emerald green eyes flicking between them. "What can I do for you?"

"Richard Evans," Sarah said bluntly, gauging Tina's reaction. "We know he frequented this place."

Tina's lips pursed, and she wiped down the counter with a rag. "Yeah, he came in here now and then. Kept to himself mostly."

"Anyone he met with regularly?" Charlie asked, leaning against the bar.

"Few people," Tina replied casually, but Sarah detected a hint of hesitation in her voice. "One guy stands out – tall, bald, nasty scar on his left cheek. Goes by the name of Jack."

"Jack who?" Sarah pressed, her pulse quickening with anticipation.

"Didn't catch a last name," Tina shrugged. "But he's bad news. Heard they were into some shady business together."

"Thanks, Tina," Charlie said, slipping her a folded bill discreetly. "You've been a great help."

"Anytime, detective," Tina replied, pocketing the money with a sly smile. "Just be careful. People around here don't take kindly to snooping."

As they retreated to a corner booth, Sarah's mind raced. "So we've got a new player – Jack," she said, her fingers tapping impatiently on the tabletop.

"Could be a major lead," Charlie agreed, his brow furrowed in thought. "We need to track him down and find out what he knows."

"Agreed," Sarah replied, her grip on the table tightening as her gambling itch flared up. She forced herself to focus on the task at hand. "But we can't rush this. We need to dig deeper, gather more intel before making our move."

"Right," Charlie nodded, concern flickering in his eyes as he noticed Sarah's tension. "Slow and steady. We'll get to the bottom of this, Sarah. We always do."

She took a deep breath, pushing her addiction to the back of her mind. "Yeah," she whispered, determination replacing doubt. "We will."

•••

The dimly lit bar hummed with activity as Sarah and Charlie exchanged a silent nod, signaling their readiness to leave. They slid out of the booth, Sarah's gaze lingering on the worn leather seats, her fingers brushing against the cracked surface. She could feel the energy of countless stories that had unfolded within these walls.

"Let's go," she whispered, her voice barely audible above the low murmur of conversation and clinking glasses.

Charlie gave her a reassuring pat on the back as they made their way towards the exit, navigating the sea of patrons nursing their drinks and sharing hushed secrets. The air felt thick with tension, a mixture of cigarette smoke and desperation clinging to every surface.

"Sarah," Charlie murmured as they stepped out into the cold night air, the door clicking shut behind them. "You did good in there."

"Thanks," she replied, her breath forming small clouds in front of her face. "I just... I can't shake this feeling that we're so close to something big."

"Trust your instincts," Charlie advised, his eyes scanning the street, always vigilant. "They've never failed you before."

A shiver ran down Sarah's spine that had little to do with the chill in the air. Her thoughts raced, darting between the information Tina had given them and her own inner demons begging to be satiated. The gambling itch clawed at her insides, but the desire for justice held it at bay.

"Charlie," she said, determination seeping into her voice. "Tomorrow, we start digging deeper. We find Jack, we uncover Richard's connections, and we bring them all down."

"Damn right," Charlie agreed, a fierce glint in his eyes. "We'll leave no stone unturned, Sarah. This case is going to be different. We'll make sure of it."

As they climbed into their car, the streetlights casting long shadows on the pavement, Sarah's resolve solidified. The gambling itch still gnawed at her, but she'd learned to compartmentalize it, to tuck it away in a dark corner of her mind. It would have to wait.

"Let's do this," she muttered, gripping the steering wheel with white-knuckled intensity as they pulled away from the curb and disappeared into the night, their focus locked on the unknown dangers that lay ahead.

3

The rain pattered against the window, a relentless reminder of the storm brewing inside Sarah Mitchell's mind. She sat in her dimly lit apartment, staring at the stack of case files spread across the table. The weight of past failures pressed down on her, heavy as the dark clouds above. Unsolved cases, careless mistakes, and lost opportunities haunted her thoughts, each one chipping away at her confidence.

"Damn it," she muttered, clenching her fists. Her gambling addiction had always been an unwelcome companion, lurking in the shadows of her life, ready to drag her down when things got tough. And they were tough now, tougher than ever before. But this time, she wouldn't let it win. This case was different; it was her chance to prove herself, to show everyone that she was more than just the screw-ups of her past.

"Sarah, you've got to get your head in the game," she whispered to herself, steeling her resolve. She had to rid herself of the ghosts haunting her career if she had any hope of moving forward. It wouldn't be easy – nothing worth doing ever was – but she owed it to herself to try.

"Alright, let's do this," she said, pushing aside her doubts and fears. She picked up the first file, her eyes scanning the pages with determination. The risks were high, she knew that, but she couldn't afford to back down. Not this time.

Deep down, she felt the familiar tug of her addiction, urging her to abandon the case for the false comfort of the casino floor. But Sarah clenched her jaw and tightened her grip on the file, refusing to succumb. No more running away, no more hiding from her demons. This was her moment to face them head-on, to reclaim her life and her career.

"Sarah, what are you doing?" a voice called from the doorway, breaking her concentration. She looked up to see her partner, Charlie, leaning against the doorframe, concern etched on his face.

"Working," she replied, straightening her back and meeting his gaze with newfound determination. "I'm going to solve this case, Charlie. I have to."

He stepped into the room, his eyes searching hers. "Are you sure you can handle it? With everything going on..."

"More than ever," she interrupted, her voice firm. "I need this, Charlie. I need to prove to myself that I can still be the detective I once was. That I can overcome my addiction and make a difference in this world."

Charlie hesitated for a moment before nodding slowly. "Alright, Sarah. I'll help you in any way I can. We'll get through this together."

"Thank you," she said, her voice soft but unwavering. "I won't let you down."

As they sat down and began sifting through the evidence, Sarah felt a flicker of hope ignite within her. It would be a long, hard road, but she was finally ready to face it head-on. And though her addiction whispered its dark promises in her ear, she knew that as long as she kept her eyes on the prize and her heart set on redemption, she could beat it – one step at a time.

•••

The neon lights of the precinct flickered overhead, casting an eerie glow on the faces of the detectives crowded around the evidence board. Sarah's fingers tightened around her cup of stale coffee as she stared at the crime scene photos and witness statements tacked to the cork surface.

"Alright, people," Captain Reynolds barked, his grizzled face set in a stern expression. "We need results on this case, and we need them now. The Commissioner is breathing down my neck, and I don't have to tell you what that means for all of us."

Sarah felt the weight of expectation settle on her shoulders like a leaden cloak. She knew that if she failed to solve this case, her career would be as good as over. And with her addiction gnawing at the edges of her resolve, the stakes had never been higher.

"Sarah," Reynolds said, his eyes fixed on her. "This is your chance to prove yourself. Don't screw it up."

"Understood, Captain," she replied, her voice steady despite the pounding in her chest. Her grip on the coffee cup tightened, knuckles turning white.

As the meeting dispersed, Sarah retreated to her desk, her thoughts racing. She could feel the familiar itch of the gambling urge creeping in, whispering sweet nothings about the thrill of the roulette wheel and the seductive allure of the blackjack table. But she pushed it away, focusing instead on the task ahead of her.

"Hey, Sarah," Charlie said, leaning against her desk. "You okay? You look a little... off."

"Fine," she snapped, immediately regretting her tone. "Sorry, Charlie. It's just... the pressure, you know?"

He nodded, concern in his eyes. "I get it. Just remember, we're all in this together. If you need help, don't hesitate to ask."

"Thanks," she murmured, forcing a smile. She knew she couldn't afford to let her addiction take over now, not when so much was on the line.

Sarah spent the rest of the day poring over the case files, each grisly detail etching itself into her mind. When night began to fall, and the precinct emptied, she could no longer ignore the siren call of her addiction.

"Damn it," she whispered, gripping the edge of her desk. Her resolve wavered, but then she thought of Reynolds' stern face and Charlie's offer of help. No, she couldn't give in. Not now.

"Come on, Sarah," she muttered, willing herself to focus. "You can do this. You have to."

With renewed determination, she dove back into the case, the specter of her addiction receding into the shadows – for now.

•••

Rain lashed against the precinct windows, the sound punctuating Sarah's thoughts like a metronome. She ran her fingers through her damp hair, shaking off droplets that stubbornly clung to her fingertips. The neon glow of the nearby casino seeped into the room, casting eerie shadows on the walls.

"Sarah," Charlie said, his voice low and concerned. "You've been at this for hours. We should call it a night."

"Can't," she replied tersely, chewing on the end of her pen. She stared at the case file spread across her desk, every gruesome detail taunting her, daring her to give in to temptation. But no, not now – not when everything was at stake.

"Listen, I know you're under a lot of pressure," Charlie continued, leaning against her desk. "But you can't let it consume you. This case is important, but so is your well-being."

"I'm fine, Charlie," she insisted, though she knew he could see right through her. The flicker of pain and disappointment in his eyes was undeniable. "I just need to focus."

"Okay," he sighed, rubbing a hand over his weary face. "But promise me one thing, Sarah: if it gets too much, talk to me. Don't try to carry it all alone."

"Promise," she whispered, the weight of her addiction bearing down on her like an anchor. But she couldn't let it win; not this time. She forced herself to concentrate on the investigation, each question and clue chipping away at her resolve.

"Have you looked closely at these phone records?" Charlie asked, tapping a finger on a sheet of paper. "There's something off about them."

"Let's check it out," Sarah replied, grateful for the distraction. They poured over the documents, their combined determination palpable in the air.

"Good catch, Charlie. This could be a lead," Sarah said, her excitement growing as she envisioned the possibility of a breakthrough.

"See? We'll crack this case together, like we always do," he reassured her, a warm smile spreading across his face. "We've got each other's backs."

"Thanks, Charlie. I needed that," Sarah admitted, her resolve strengthening with each passing moment. She balled up her fists, gritting her teeth. The addiction would not win today; she wouldn't let it.

"Anytime, partner," Charlie replied, clapping her on the shoulder. "Now, let's get to work."

•••

The room was dim, the only light coming from a single bulb swinging above. Sarah stood in front of a corkboard, studying the crime scene photos pinned to it. "We need to dig deeper," she muttered, her voice resolute.

"Into what?" Charlie asked, leaning against the wall, arms crossed over his chest.

"Connections. Motives. The things people hide." She didn't look away from the board, her eyes scanning each image as if searching for a hidden clue. "Someone out there knows something, and I'm going to find them."

"Sarah, you know this case could get dangerous, right?" Charlie's concern was evident in his tone, but he knew better than to try to dissuade her.

"Of course. But I'm not backing down," she replied, finally meeting his gaze. "I can't afford to fail again."

"Alright. Just remember we're in this together." He pushed off the wall and joined her by the board.

"Did you notice this?" Sarah pointed at a picture of the victim's apartment. "That's an expensive painting. Way out of the victim's price range."

"Maybe they had a secret benefactor," Charlie suggested, eyebrows raised.

"Or maybe they were involved in something they shouldn't have been." A fire burned in Sarah's eyes as she stared at the photo. "We need to track down the origin of that painting and see where it leads us."

"Could be a dead end," Charlie cautioned, but Sarah shook her head.

"Even if it is, we can't ignore any potential lead. Remember, we're dealing with someone who's already killed once. They won't hesitate to do it again if they feel threatened." Her hands balled into fists at her sides, her knuckles turning white.

"Alright, let's follow it up," Charlie agreed, pulling out his phone to start researching the painting. "But be careful, Sarah. Whoever we're dealing with might not want these secrets brought to light."

"Neither do I," she murmured, her heart pounding in her chest. Every lead they pursued could bring her face-to-face with the uncomfortable truths she'd spent her life trying to outrun. But Sarah knew that this case was her chance at redemption, and she refused to let it slip through her fingers.

"Sarah?" Charlie's voice cut through her thoughts, his eyes searching hers for any sign of distress. "You good?"

"Better than ever," she replied, a steely determination settling over her features. "Let's get to work."

•••

The dim light of the computer screen cast a blue hue across Sarah's face, her eyes scanning every article and forum post she could find about the mysterious painting. Her fingers danced across the keyboard, pulling up images and auction records in an attempt to trace its history.

"Got something." Charlie leaned over her shoulder, pointing to an auction listing from six years ago. "Looks like it was sold by a private collector."

"Can we find out who they are?" Sarah asked, her voice barely above a whisper. The need for answers gnawed at her insides, fueling her determination to unravel this case.

"Let me see what I can dig up," Charlie replied, opening another browser window and diving into the depths of the internet.

As Sarah continued to search, her mind wandered back to the crime scene, the victim's lifeless body sprawled on the floor—a reminder of the stakes involved and the danger lurking around every corner. She clenched her jaw, refusing to let fear or doubt cloud her judgment.

"Sarah?" Charlie interrupted her thoughts again. "I found our collector. Name's Arthur Prescott. Lives just outside the city."

"Any connection to our victim?" she asked, hope flickering in her eyes.

"None that I can see," Charlie admitted, his brow furrowed in frustration. "But there's something off about this guy. Reclusive, wealthy, no known occupation. And he has a penchant for collecting controversial art."

"Sounds like we need to pay Mr. Prescott a visit." Sarah stood up, her spine stiff with resolve as she grabbed her jacket. "We need to know if he had any involvement in this murder."

"Agreed," Charlie said, nodding solemnly. "But remember, we're treading on dangerous ground here. We can't afford to make any mistakes."

"Understood," she replied, slipping on her jacket. "This case is my chance to prove myself, Charlie. To show everyone that I'm not a screw-up."

"Sarah," he said, placing a reassuring hand on her shoulder. "I've always believed in you. And I know you'll solve this case. Just remember to trust your instincts and stay focused."

"Thanks, Charlie," she whispered, her heart swelling with gratitude for his unwavering support. Together, they would face the darkness and bring justice to light.

•••

The rain pelted the windshield as Sarah parked her car outside the gated entrance to Arthur Prescott's expansive property. She glanced over at Charlie, who was flipping through his notepad, double-checking their collected information.

"Are we ready for this?" she asked, her hands gripping the steering wheel tightly.

"Ready as we'll ever be," he replied, meeting her gaze with determination.

Sarah took a deep breath and stepped out of the car, the cold rain immediately soaking through her clothes. The weight of her past failures pressed down on her shoulders like an invisible burden, but she steeled herself, refusing to let it hinder her progress.

Together, they approached the mansion's massive front door, its dark wood weathered from years of neglect. As Sarah rang the doorbell, she felt a shiver run down her spine. Unsettling secrets lurked behind these walls, and she was determined to uncover them.

"Detective Mitchell, Detective Thompson," a smooth voice greeted them as the door creaked open, revealing a tall, thin man with slicked-back gray hair. "Mr. Prescott has been expecting you."

Sarah exchanged a glance with Charlie before stepping inside, her senses on high alert. The opulent foyer reeked of wealth and decay, the scent of old money mingling with the faint odor of dampness.

"Please, follow me," the man said, leading them down a dimly lit hallway lined with eerie, provocative paintings. Sarah studied each one intently, searching for any clue that might connect Prescott to their victim.

"Detective Mitchell?" Charlie whispered, noticing her intense focus on the artwork. "You okay?"

"Fine," she muttered, barely audible above the echoing footsteps. "Just looking for anything out of place."

"Understood."

The chilling atmosphere weighed heavily on her chest, threatening to suffocate her resolve. But Sarah refused to let the darkness consume her, instead feeding off its energy to fuel her determination. She would not fail this time; she couldn't.

"Here we are," their guide announced, opening a set of double doors to reveal a grand library filled with floor-to-ceiling bookshelves. "Mr. Prescott will be with you shortly."

"Thank you," Sarah said tersely, scanning the room for any signs of criminal activity or hidden secrets. Every fiber of her being screamed that something was amiss, and she wouldn't rest until she uncovered it.

"Sarah, look at this," Charlie hissed, pulling a leather-bound journal from a nearby shelf. "It's full of names and dates—some sort of coded ledger."

"Let me see," she said, taking the journal from him and flipping through the pages, her eyes widening with each cryptic entry. This could be the break they needed, the key to unlocking the truth behind their victim's death.

"Detectives?" Arthur Prescott's voice cut through the tension like a knife, startling them both. "I understand you have some questions for me."

"Indeed, we do, Mr. Prescott," Sarah replied, her heart pounding in her chest as she clutched the journal tightly. She locked eyes with the enigmatic collector, her gaze unwavering and resolute.

"Ask away," he said, an unsettling smile forming on his thin lips.

"Rest assured, Mr. Prescott," Sarah's voice was steady and determined, "we'll get to the bottom of this, no matter what it takes."

•••

Rain pounded the windowpane as Sarah sat at her desk, hunched over a stack of evidence photos. The dark circles under her eyes betrayed her exhaustion, but she couldn't afford to rest – not yet. She scrutinized every detail, desperate to find the missing piece that would unravel the case.

"Another late night?" Charlie leaned against the doorway, concern etched on his face.

"Can't help it," Sarah muttered, fingers tapping rhythmically on the tabletop. "I'm close, Charlie. I can feel it."

"Sarah, you need sleep." He placed a hand on her shoulder, but she shrugged it off.

"Sleep's for quitters," she retorted, forcing a smile that didn't quite reach her eyes.

"Alright, alright," Charlie conceded, knowing better than to push. "Just take care of yourself, okay?"

"Promise." The word felt heavy on her tongue, weighed down by unspoken fears and memories of past failures.

As Charlie left the room, Sarah's gaze drifted to the corner of her desk where an unopened envelope lay. Her fingers itched to tear it open, to feel the familiar thrill of placing a bet on a surefire winner. But she clenched her fist, nails digging into her palm. No. Not this time. This case was her priority – her redemption.

She turned back to the photos, her resolve hardening like steel. It was then that she noticed something – a tiny speck of red on the victim's sleeve. Blood? A lead?

"Charlie!" she called, excitement igniting in her chest. "Get in here!"

He rushed back in, eyebrows raised in anticipation. "What is it?"

"Look," she pointed at the photo. "We missed this before. It could be our break."

"Nice catch," Charlie grinned, admiration shining in his eyes. "Let's run with it."

As they dove into the new lead, Sarah's thoughts lingered on the unopened envelope. The urge to gamble gnawed at her insides like a ravenous beast, but she fought it back with every ounce of strength she possessed.

"Focus," she whispered to herself, eyes trained on the task at hand. "You can do this."

And for the first time in a long while, she believed it.

•••

The sun dipped below the horizon, casting long shadows across Sarah's cluttered desk. Her eyes burned as she scanned the case files again, each grisly detail sharpening her resolve. Charlie leaned against the doorframe, watching her intently.

"Sarah," he said, a note of concern in his voice, "you've been at this for hours. Take a break."

"Can't." She shook her head, fingers tapping on the desktop. "I need to find something we missed."

"Hey," Charlie stepped forward, placing a reassuring hand on her shoulder. "We'll get there. Together."

"Thanks, Charlie." She offered him a small, tired smile before refocusing on the documents sprawled across her workspace.

"Remember the Delaney case?" He asked, trying to lighten the mood. "When you were so obsessed with finding that missing piece, you accidentally knocked over your coffee right onto the evidence?"

"Ha," Sarah huffed, rolling her eyes. "Barely salvaged that lead."

"Exactly. And we still closed that case. Don't lose yourself in this one."

"Right." She sighed, rubbing her temples. "It's just... I need to make this work. For me. To prove I can beat my own demons."

Charlie squeezed her shoulder gently. "I know you can. You're stronger than you think."

As they shared a moment of understanding, Sarah's phone buzzed on the table – a text from an unknown number. Her heart raced, recognizing it as the allure of a high-stakes gamble whispered through the digital ether.

"Everything okay?" Charlie asked, catching her hesitation.

"Fine," she lied, slipping the phone back into her pocket. "Just the usual spam."

"Alright, then." He eyed her skeptically but didn't press further. "Let's keep working."

"Right." The word tasted like ash in her mouth as the temptation gnawed at her resolve.

"Wait," Sarah's eyes locked onto a line in the coroner's report. "This... this is it. The connection between the victims."

"Let me see." Charlie leaned in, scanning the page. "Damn, you're good. This changes everything."

"Thanks." Sarah exhaled, relief washing over her as the urge to gamble receded like a tide. "We're on the right track now."

"Absolutely." His pride in her was evident. "You got this, Sarah."

"Damn right I do." She clenched her jaw, newfound confidence surging through her veins. "I'm all in on this case – no distractions, no weaknesses. I will solve this."

And with that declaration, Sarah pushed aside the pull of her addiction, ready to face the challenges ahead and prove herself as the top-notch detective she always knew she could be.

4

The sun dipped below the horizon, casting long shadows across Sarah's cluttered desk. Her eyes burned as she scanned the case files again, each grisly detail sharpening her resolve. Charlie leaned against the doorframe, watching her intently.

"Sarah," he said, a note of concern in his voice, "you've been at this for hours. Take a break."

"Can't." She shook her head, fingers tapping on the desktop. "I need to find something we missed."

"Hey," Charlie stepped forward, placing a reassuring hand on her shoulder. "We'll get there. Together."

"Thanks, Charlie." She offered him a small, tired smile before refocusing on the documents sprawled across her workspace.

"Remember the Delaney case?" He asked, trying to lighten the mood. "When you were so obsessed with finding that missing piece, you accidentally knocked over your coffee right onto the evidence?"

"Ha," Sarah huffed, rolling her eyes. "Barely salvaged that lead."

"Exactly. And we still closed that case. Don't lose yourself in this one."

"Right." She sighed, rubbing her temples. "It's just... I need to make this work. For me. To prove I can beat my own demons."

Charlie squeezed her shoulder gently. "I know you can. You're stronger than you think."

As they shared a moment of understanding, Sarah's phone buzzed on the table – a text from an unknown number. Her heart raced, recognizing it as the allure of a high-stakes gamble whispered through the digital ether.

"Everything okay?" Charlie asked, catching her hesitation.

"Fine," she lied, slipping the phone back into her pocket. "Just the usual spam."

"Alright, then." He eyed her skeptically but didn't press further. "Let's keep working."

"Right." The word tasted like ash in her mouth as the temptation gnawed at her resolve.

"Wait," Sarah's eyes locked onto a line in the coroner's report. "This... this is it. The connection between the victims."

"Let me see." Charlie leaned in, scanning the page. "Damn, you're good. This changes everything."

"Thanks." Sarah exhaled, relief washing over her as the urge to gamble receded like a tide. "We're on the right track now."

"Absolutely." His pride in her was evident. "You got this, Sarah."

"Damn right I do." She clenched her jaw, newfound confidence surging through her veins. "I'm all in on this case – no distractions, no weaknesses. I will solve this."

And with that declaration, Sarah pushed aside the pull of her addiction, ready to face the challenges ahead and prove herself as the top-notch detective she always knew she could be.

•••

"Detective Sarah Mitchell," Sarah said, extending a hand towards Tina. Her voice wavered like a gambler's last chip, desperate for a win. "This is my partner, Detective Charlie Reynolds. We're working the Richard Evans case."

"Ah, the famous detectives," Tina drawled, her fingers wrapping around Sarah's in a firm grip. The chill of the glass she'd been polishing still lingered on her skin. "Heard a thing or two about you."

Sarah caught Charlie's gaze, his eyes narrowing beneath furrowed brows. They both knew Tina's reputation – if there was any dirt to dig up, she'd already have it under her nails.

"Nice to meet you, Tina," Charlie said, offering his own handshake. His grip was steady, betraying none of the uncertainty that gnawed at his insides. What new secrets could this case uncover? He'd seen it all, or so he thought.

"Likewise," Tina replied, sizing them up with an appraising eye. Her gaze flickered between them, the curiosity and skepticism in those emerald orbs reflecting the bar's neon lights like a kaleidoscope.

"Mind if we ask you a few questions?" Sarah asked, trying to sound nonchalant as she fished a notebook from her pocket. Would this gamble pay off? She couldn't afford another mistake, not when her career and sanity teetered on the edge.

"Shoot," Tina said, leaning against the bar with a playful smirk. The clink of glasses punctuated her words, layers of noise weaving a tapestry of town life around them. She tilted her head, studying them as if they were specimens in a petri dish. "Let's see what I can do for you."

•••

"Listen, Tina," Sarah began, her voice tinged with wariness, "we've heard you're good at collecting gossip, but we need something more concrete."

"Concrete?" Tina scoffed, crossing her arms. "Darlin', I know this town like the back of my hand. You'd be surprised what people let slip in a place like this." She gestured around the dimly lit bar, the low hum of conversations and laughter melding with the faint aroma of cigarette smoke and stale beer.

"Alright then," Charlie said, casting a doubtful glance at Sarah before shifting his focus back to Tina. "Tell us something about Richard Evans that might actually help our case."

Tina leaned in closer, her crimson curls framing her face like a halo of fire. "You didn't hear it from me, but Richard had a little somethin' goin' on with his neighbor, Mrs. Johnson. Retired schoolteacher she is, but apparently still spry enough for late-night rendezvous."

Sarah's eyes widened at the revelation, while Charlie's mouth formed a tight line. The detective's mind raced, thoughts tumbling over one another as she grappled with this new information. Was this just small-town gossip or an essential piece of their puzzle?

"Mrs. Johnson, huh?" Charlie muttered, scribbling down the name in his own notebook. He glanced up, his steely eyes meeting Tina's. "Is there anything else you can tell us?"

"Perhaps," Tina said coyly, her lips curling into a knowing smile. "But first, I need your word that my name won't be mentioned. I value my customers' trust, after all."

"Of course," Sarah assured her, her voice steady now. "Discretion is part of our job."

"Good," Tina replied, satisfied. "Now, let me see... What else do I have for you?"

As they listened to Tina's revelations, Sarah couldn't help but feel a spark of hope ignite deep within her. Maybe this would be the break she so desperately needed – the one that would finally put her gambling demons and streak of bad luck to rest.

•••

Sarah's heart pounded as she shared a glance with Charlie. It was as if Tina had suddenly flipped on a light switch, illuminating the dark corners of their investigation. She recalled reading about Mr. Johnson's past in the case file – a string of petty thefts and a history of violence.

"Mr. Johnson," she murmured, her voice barely audible over the bar's ambient din. "He's got a record."

"Right," Charlie agreed, his eyes narrowing as he processed the significance. He leaned closer to Sarah, speaking in hushed tones. "If he knew about the affair... that's motive alright."

"Exactly," Sarah replied, biting her lower lip as her mind raced. This could be the lead they were waiting for – a real suspect, someone they could pursue with tangible evidence.

Tina, having caught the tail end of their exchange, leaned forward, resting an elbow on the bar top. "You two look like you've just struck gold," she observed, her emerald green eyes twinkling with amusement. "But wait, there's more."

"More?" Charlie raised an eyebrow, his curiosity piqued.

"Richard had a falling out with his business partner, Mark Thompson," Tina divulged, her voice low and conspiratorial. "Apparently, it was over some shady deal involving stolen goods. Word is, things got pretty ugly between them."

"Stolen goods?" Sarah repeated, feeling a thrill surge through her. This case was finally starting to take shape; the murky waters clearing as potential suspects emerged from the depths.

"Thompson, huh?" Charlie mused, scribbling down the name alongside Mr. Johnson's. "That gives us two solid leads."

"Seems our friend Richard made quite a few enemies," Sarah thought, her gaze fixed on the now-empty whiskey glass in front of her, the ghost of its bitter taste lingering on her tongue.

"Indeed," Tina agreed, her expression somber for the first time since their arrival. "It's a shame, really. But I suppose that's what happens when you mix with the wrong crowd."

"Thanks, Tina," Charlie said sincerely, grateful for her invaluable assistance. "We'll be sure to look into these leads."

"Good luck," she replied, nodding at them both. "And remember – mum's the word."

"Of course," Sarah promised, her resolve solidified. With these new leads, she could finally piece together the truth. They had a real shot at solving this case, and she refused to let it slip through her fingers.

●●●

The amber glow of the bar's neon sign cast shadows on Sarah's face, as she frowned in contemplation. Beads of condensation slid down her glass, mirroring the tension that hung heavy in the air.

"Mark Thompson," Charlie muttered, his voice gravelly and low. "Could be a solid lead."

Sarah nodded, her eyes narrowing as she envisioned the potential suspect. Her fingers drummed on the sticky counter, each tap punctuating her thoughts. *Angry partner... stolen goods... it all adds up.*

"Wait," Tina interjected, her emerald eyes gleaming with the promise of more information. "There's someone else you should know about."

"Who?" Sarah asked, leaning closer.

"James," Tina whispered, glancing around the bar to ensure no one was eavesdropping. "He's a bit of an enigma, but he's been seen arguing with Richard multiple times right here in this very bar."

"James?" Charlie questioned, his brow furrowing. "Any last name?"

"Nobody knows," Tina replied, shaking her head. "Just goes by James."

"Interesting," Sarah mused, feeling the addictive pull of a new lead tugging at her mind. She imagined the mysterious man, his motives hidden behind a veil of secrecy. *Who are you, James? And what do you have to hide?*

"Keep an eye out for him," Tina advised, her gaze darting across the room.

"Will do," Charlie agreed, making a mental note of this elusive figure. "Thanks, Tina."

"Anything to help," she responded, a sly smile playing on her lips.

As the pieces of the puzzle began to fit together, Sarah's heart pounded in anticipation. The game was afoot, and she was ready to play her part. No longer would her past failures define her; she'd prove herself, once and for all.

"Let's get to work," she declared, meeting Charlie's gaze with determination.

"Couldn't agree more," he replied, a hint of pride in his eyes. Together, they'd uncover the truth, no matter where it led. The night was young, and justice waited for no one.

•••

The low hum of conversation filled the air, punctuated by the clink of glassware. Sarah's pulse quickened as she gripped her pen, scribbling down the leads Tina had provided. Charlie, his eyes alight with excitement, mirrored her fervor as he jotted notes on his own pad.

"Mrs. Johnson's affair, Mark Thompson's shady business, and this James guy," Sarah mused, her mind racing. "We've got some solid leads here."

"Finally, the break we needed," Charlie agreed, his gruff voice tinged with hope. "So many threads to pull."

Tina watched them with a mixture of amusement and pride, her arms folded across her chest. "I told you I knew some things," she said, smirking. "Glad I could help."

"More than you know," Sarah replied, locking eyes with the fiery redhead. "But we need to ask you a favor."

"Sure, what is it?" Tina inquired, tilting her head.

"Keep our meeting a secret," Charlie interjected. "We don't want anyone to know you've been talking to us."

"Of course," Tina nodded solemnly. "Mum's the word."

"Thank you, Tina," Sarah said, sincerity lacing her words. She glanced at Charlie, who gave her a reassuring nod. It was time to leave the bar and start chasing these new leads.

"Alright, let's get out of here," Charlie declared, standing up and pocketing his notepad. "We've got work to do."

"Couldn't agree more," Sarah responded, feeling a newfound determination surging through her veins. The weight of past failures seemed to lighten, replaced by a burning desire to bring justice to light.

"Good luck," Tina whispered as they turned to leave, her voice barely audible over the din of the bar.

"Thanks," Charlie replied, offering her a grateful smile. "We'll need it."

The night beckoned, its dark embrace promising answers to questions long unanswered. As Sarah stepped through the door and into the crisp evening air, she felt alive, ready to face whatever challenges lay ahead. The game was on, and this time, she wouldn't lose.

•••

The door creaked shut behind them, cutting off the boisterous clamor of the bar. The cool night air was a balm on their flushed faces, crisp and invigorating. Streetlamps cast pools of yellow light onto the damp pavement, reflecting in the puddles from an earlier rain. The city hummed with life, but for a moment, they stood alone in a pocket of stillness.

"Didn't see that coming," Charlie mused, his breath visible in the chilly air.

"Me neither," Sarah admitted, her eyes locked on Charlie's. Shadows danced across his face, betraying the emotions he tried to keep hidden.

"Feels like we're finally getting somewhere," he said with a half-smile, a glint of optimism playing in his eyes. Sarah nodded, feeling the weight of past failures begin to lift.

"Let's not waste any time," she urged, her mind racing with possibilities. "We need to follow up on these leads."

"Agreed." Charlie pulled out his notepad, flipping through the pages. "Mrs. Johnson first?"

"Sounds good." Sarah's fingers itched to start digging, to peel back the layers of secrets surrounding Richard Evans. She clenched her fists, determined to prove herself as a capable detective.

"Alright then," Charlie said, stuffing his notepad back into his pocket. He gave Sarah a reassuring pat on the back, the warmth of his touch lingering even after he withdrew his hand. "Let's hit the road."

"Right behind you," Sarah replied, her voice steady and resolute. She followed Charlie as he navigated the dark streets, the city unfolding around them like an intricate puzzle waiting to be solved.

As they walked, Sarah's thoughts drifted to the looming specter of her gambling addiction. Would this case be her redemption, or would her demons continue to haunt her? She shook her head, pushing the doubt away. Now was not the time for self-pity; she had a job to do, and come hell or high water, she would see it through.

"Hey," Charlie called out, pulling Sarah from her reverie. "You alright?"

"Fine," she said, forcing a tight-lipped smile. "Just...ready to crack this case wide open."

"Me too." Charlie's eyes met hers, a spark of determination igniting between them. Together, they pressed on into the night, chasing justice under the watchful gaze of the moon.

5

The sun cast a golden glow on the sand as Sarah and Charlie pulled up to Alicia Davis' luxurious beachfront property. Waves crashed rhythmically against the shore, contrasting with the tension that hung heavy in the air. Sarah's fingers tapped nervously on the steering wheel, her mind racing with thoughts of Richard's murder and the tangled web of suspects.

"Ready?" Charlie asked, his salt-and-pepper hair ruffling in the sea breeze.

"Let's do this," Sarah replied, her short brown hair whipped back as she stepped out of the car.

They approached the door, a sense of unease settling in Sarah's gut. Knocking firmly, they waited for Alicia to answer. The door creaked open, revealing a distraught woman with long blonde hair and red, puffy eyes.

"Detective Mitchell, Detective Reynolds," Alicia said, her voice trembling. "Come in."

"Thank you, Mrs. Davis," Sarah replied, stepping inside the opulent foyer, her keen eyes scanning the surroundings.

As they entered, Sarah noticed the expensive artwork adorning the walls and the high ceilings that accentuated the grandeur of the home. She couldn't help but think about how her gambling addiction had left her with nothing close to this kind of luxury.

"Please, have a seat," Alicia gestured towards the plush couches in the living area. Her body language was tense, her movements stiff and guarded.

"Thank you," Charlie said, taking a seat. Sarah followed suit, trying to put Alicia at ease with a small smile.

"Mrs. Davis, we're here to ask some questions about your husband, Richard," Sarah began, her voice steady.

"Of course," Alicia whispered, wiping away fresh tears.

"Did Richard have any enemies that you know of? Anyone who might want to harm him?" Sarah asked.

Alicia hesitated, glancing nervously around the room. "I – I don't know," she stammered. "He had some business associates who didn't always agree with him, but I never thought they'd go this far."

"Can you think of any reason someone would want to hurt him?" Charlie pressed gently.

"Nothing comes to mind," Alicia replied, her eyes darting between the detectives, as if searching for reassurance.

Sarah's thoughts roiled beneath the surface as she studied Alicia's face. She couldn't shake the feeling that there was more to this story than they were being told. She needed to find out what Richard was involved in, and how deep his estranged wife's connection went.

"Thank you for your cooperation, Mrs. Davis," Sarah said, her tone firm. "We'll be in touch if we have any further questions."

"Please," Alicia whispered, her voice cracking. "Find whoever did this."

As they left the residence, the ocean breeze carried a chilling reminder that danger lurked around every corner in this case. Sarah felt a renewed determination to uncover the truth, no matter the cost.

•••

Once inside Alicia's home, Sarah took in the opulent surroundings. The sun dipped low in the sky, casting a golden glow over the lavish furnishings and pristine white walls. She couldn't help but think of her own cramped apartment, cluttered with takeout cartons and unpaid bills. The contrast was almost too much to bear.

"Mrs. Davis," Charlie began, his voice gentle. "We need to ask you about your relationship with Richard. Can you think of any reason why someone would want him dead?"

Alicia's gaze darted around the room as she bit her lip. "Our marriage had its ups and downs, but I loved him," she whispered, her voice quivering. "I wish I could tell you more."

"Any disagreements or problems between the two of you recently?" Sarah asked, watching Alicia closely.

"Nothing out of the ordinary," Alicia replied, wringing her hands together. "Just the usual marital issues."

Sarah's gut told her there was something more. She felt her gambling addiction itch, like an old wound begging to be scratched. It was a high-stakes bluff, but she couldn't resist the urge to press further. "Are you sure there's nothing else you can tell us, Mrs. Davis? We're here to help."

Alicia's eyes widened, and she looked over her shoulder as if expecting someone to burst through the door at any moment. Her breaths came in short, panicked gasps. "I – I think someone's been following me," she stammered.

"Following you?" Charlie echoed, his brow furrowing with concern.

"Since Richard's death, I've noticed strange cars parked outside my house. People watching me when I go out," Alicia admitted, her voice barely audible.

"Mrs. Davis, we'll do everything we can to ensure your safety," Sarah reassured her, trying to calm the rising tide of panic in the room. "We'll have officers keep an eye on your house and monitor any suspicious activity."

"Thank you," Alicia whispered, her gaze darting between them. "I just — I don't know who to trust anymore."

Sarah exchanged a glance with Charlie, their shared concern for Alicia's well-being palpable in the air. As they left the luxurious beachfront home, Sarah couldn't help but wonder if the glittering facade hid secrets darker than she could imagine. It was a question that she knew would haunt her until she found the truth.

•••

A shaft of sunlight pierced the room, illuminating the dust motes that swirled in the air. The smell of salt and seaweed carried on the ocean breeze. Sarah's eyes caught a glimpse of a framed photograph on a side table, depicting Alicia and Richard, tanned and smiling, their arms entwined as they stood on a white-sand beach.

"Mrs. Davis," Sarah said softly, gesturing to the photo. "Did Richard's business dealings ever cause you concern? You must have been aware of his connections to less-than-legal activities."

Alicia's gaze flicked to the picture, then back to Sarah. Her fingers fidgeted with the hem of her blouse, eyes darting away for a moment before she spoke.

"Richard... he had a complicated past. And yes, I knew about some of it." She hesitated, her voice barely more than a whisper. "He was involved in money laundering, drug trafficking... things I never wanted to be a part of."

Charlie leaned forward, elbows on knees, his stare unyielding. "And you didn't think this might be relevant information for us, Mrs. Davis?"

Alicia's jaw tightened, her eyes shimmering with unshed tears. "I didn't want to believe that any of that could have led to... to this." She swallowed hard, her breath shaky. "I thought we left that life behind."

Sarah's heart clenched at Alicia's vulnerability, the weight of her regrets evident. But she couldn't ignore the nagging suspicion that there was still more to uncover. She studied Alicia, her thoughts racing, trying to find the right words to coax the truth out of her.

"Anything you tell us can help us find Richard's killer, Alicia," she urged gently, using her first name to establish a connection. "We're here to protect you and bring justice for your husband. You need to trust us."

Alicia's eyes met Sarah's, her gaze searching for sincerity. After a moment, she nodded, tears streaming down her cheeks as she whispered, "I'll tell you everything I know."

•••

Alicia's trembling hands gripped the edge of the coffee table, her knuckles a stark white. Sarah watched her closely, noting the fear and desperation in her eyes. "Alicia," she said softly, "did you know about Richard's activities? Did you have any involvement?"

"Absolutely not," Alicia spat, her voice cracking. "I was kept in the dark, I swear! He never told me anything."

"Can you think of anyone who would want to hurt him?" Charlie asked, his voice gruff but patient.

"Everyone he dealt with... they were all ruthless. But I don't know specific names." She shook her head, tears streaming down her cheeks. "I didn't ask questions, I just... tried to keep my distance."

Sarah sighed, her instincts telling her there was more beneath the surface, but the wall of distress Alicia had built around herself seemed impenetrable. "Alright, Alicia. If you remember anything else, please give us a call immediately."

"Promise me you'll find who did this," Alicia whispered, her voice barely audible. "Promise me you'll make them pay."

"We'll do our best, Mrs. Davis," Charlie reassured her, his tone softening. "We won't rest until we find the truth."

Charlie held open the door for Sarah as they stepped out of the lavish beachfront home. The salty ocean breeze whipped through Sarah's hair, the spray stinging her cheeks. She blinked against the wind, her thoughts heavy with the weight of unsolved secrets.

"Tom Spencer," Charlie muttered, checking his notes. "He owns 'Iron Fist Fitness,' right? Maybe he knows something."

"Let's hope so," Sarah agreed, her mind racing. As they climbed into their car, the sun dipped below the horizon, casting long shadows across the sand. The world seemed to hold its breath, waiting for the darkness to swallow it whole.

"Something's not right," Sarah whispered, her fingers drumming against the steering wheel. "Alicia knows more than she's letting on."

"Maybe," Charlie conceded, staring out the window at the fading light. "But our job is to follow the leads, not speculate on her guilt or innocence."

"Right." Sarah nodded, the engine roaring to life beneath her hands. "Let's go pay Tom Spencer a visit."

As the car pulled away from Alicia's residence, the ocean's relentless waves crashed against the shore, whispering the secrets of the deep. And for a moment, Sarah imagined herself diving into the cold water, searching for the truth hidden beneath the surface. But the truth was always farther away than it seemed, buried beneath layers of deception and betrayal. She would need to keep digging, relentlessly, until justice was served.

•••

The heavy thud of fists on punching bags filled the air, mixing with the grunts and groans of exertion. Iron Fist Fitness was alive with the sounds of sweat and perseverance, a temple to the human body's potential. Sarah's eyes scanned the room, settling on a muscular man with tattoos covering his arms, instructing a client on proper boxing technique. Tom Spencer.

"Wait here," Charlie said, leaning against a nearby wall. "We'll approach him together once he's done."

Sarah nodded, her gaze fixated on Tom. She studied his movements, the way he glided around his client, demonstrating each punch with precision. It was hard to imagine that this man was once involved in Richard Evans' criminal world. But people changed, didn't they? Or did they simply become better at hiding their true nature?

"Alright, let's go," Charlie murmured, pushing away from the wall as Tom finished up with his client.

"Mr. Spencer?" Sarah called out, striding toward him with confidence.

"Detective Mitchell and Detective Reynolds," she introduced them, flashing her badge. "We're investigating the murder of Richard Evans and would like to ask you a few questions."

Tom's brow furrowed, his eyes flickering with something akin to concern. "Sure, what do you need to know?"

"Can you tell us about any past connections you had with Richard? And were you involved in any illegal activities together?" Charlie asked, his voice steady and calm.

Tom hesitated for a moment, then sighed. "Look, I'm not proud of my past. Yes, I knew Richard. We were partners in some... unsavory ventures. But that was a long time ago. I've turned my life around since then."

"Unsavory ventures?" Sarah echoed, her mind racing with the implications.

"Drugs, mainly," Tom admitted, his voice low. "But I got out of that life. I served my time, and now I'm just trying to make an honest living."

"Did you have any contact with Richard recently? Anything that could connect you to his murder?" Charlie pressed on.

"No," Tom said firmly, shaking his head. "I haven't spoken to him in years. I wanted nothing to do with him or his world anymore."

Sarah studied Tom's face, searching for any hint of deception. He seemed genuine, but she couldn't shake the feeling that there was more to this story than met the eye. And it was her job to uncover it, no matter how deep the lies went.

"Thank you for your cooperation, Mr. Spencer," Sarah said finally, stepping back. "We may need to speak with you again during our investigation."

"Of course," Tom replied, his eyes downcast. "Anything to help find Richard's killer."

As they exited the gym, Sarah's thoughts swirled like a hurricane, threatening to sweep her away. She glanced over at Charlie, who seemed equally lost in thought.

"Something's not adding up," she muttered, her hand gripping the door handle of the car. "There's more to this than just a simple murder."

"Agreed," Charlie sighed, sliding into the driver's seat. "But we won't find answers just by standing here."

"Right," Sarah nodded, determination settling in her bones. "Let's get to work."

The truth was buried beneath layers of secrets and betrayal, but Sarah knew one thing for certain: she wouldn't rest until justice was served.

• • •

The fluorescent lights of the gym flickered, casting a harsh glow on Tom Spencer's sweat-soaked face. He stood, his breath heavy, in front of Sarah and Charlie, who held a manila folder stuffed with incriminating evidence.

"Look, Mr. Spencer," Charlie said, opening the folder to reveal surveillance photos of Tom and Richard together. "We've got you meeting with Richard at multiple known criminal hotspots."

Tom swallowed hard, visibly shaken by the images. His voice trembled as he denied any involvement. "That was a long time ago. I didn't have anything to do with his illegal activities."

Sarah narrowed her eyes, catching the edge of fear in Tom's voice. She leaned in closer, pressing him further. "Then why were you seen leaving Richard's office just two weeks ago?"

"Coincidence," Tom shot back weakly. "I needed some paperwork for the gym. That's all."

"Your fingerprints were found on a weapon used in one of Richard's deals," Charlie continued, his tone ice-cold. "You can't deny that."

"I... I..." Tom stuttered, his facade crumbling under the weight of their evidence. The room felt like it was closing in on him, his heart pounding in his ears.

"Tom," Sarah said softly, her gaze piercing through him, "it's time to come clean."

He hesitated for a moment, then hung his head in defeat.

"Alright," he whispered. "Yes, I was involved with Richard. We were partners in crime, dealing drugs, laundering money – the whole thing. But I swear I left that life behind when I opened this gym."

"Did Richard ever threaten to expose your past?" Charlie asked, watching Tom closely.

"Maybe once or twice," Tom admitted, wiping the sweat from his brow. "But I never thought he'd actually do it."

"Could someone else have found out about your past?" Sarah asked, her mind racing with possibilities.

"Maybe," Tom said, his eyes darting nervously around the room. "But I don't know who would want to hurt me like this."

"Whoever it is," Charlie said, closing the folder and pocketing it, "they've put you right in the middle of a murder investigation."

"Please," Tom begged, desperation in his eyes, "I've worked so hard to build a new life for myself. Don't let them destroy it."

"Your fate depends on the truth, Mr. Spencer," Sarah said, her voice unwavering. "If you help us find Richard's killer, we'll do everything we can to protect you."

As they walked out of the gym, Sarah's mind swirled with questions. How deep did Tom's connections go? What other secrets were hiding beneath the surface?

Only time would reveal the answers, but one thing was certain: their investigation had just taken a dangerous turn.

•••

"Tom," Sarah began, her voice firm but empathetic, "we need to know everything you can remember about Richard's dealings. Any names, places, or incidents that might help us uncover the truth."

The gym echoed with the sound of weights clanking and the steady rhythm of footsteps on treadmills. Underneath the fluorescent lights, Tom's face looked weary, his tattoos a stark contrast to his pale skin.

"Look," he sighed, rubbing the back of his neck, "it's been years since we were involved in that stuff. I don't have much to offer."

"Anything could be helpful," Charlie chimed in, leaning against a nearby punching bag. "Even if it seems insignificant."

Tom hesitated, his eyes flicking between the two detectives.

"All right," he relented. "There was this one guy, went by the name of 'Razor.' He was our main contact for the drug trafficking."

Sarah's mind raced, trying to commit every detail to memory. Razor – a potential lead. She felt a small surge of adrenaline, the familiar thrill of a gamble.

"Have you had any contact with him recently?" she asked.

"No," Tom replied, shaking his head. "Not since I got out of prison and started this place. I cut all ties."

"Is there anyone else we should know about?" Charlie questioned, his eyes scanning the gym as if searching for hidden threats.

"Maybe some old associates," Tom admitted, his voice barely audible above the din of the gym. "But I've stayed away from those people. I swear."

"Thank you, Tom," Sarah said, nodding. "We'll be in touch if we have more questions."

As they exited the gym, the cool evening air hit their faces like a welcome reprieve from the stuffy atmosphere inside. The sun dipped below the horizon, casting long shadows across the parking lot.

"Where do we go from here?" Charlie mused, his salt-and-pepper hair glinting in the fading light.

Sarah's thoughts raced, her mind a whirlwind of possibilities.

"We need to dig deeper into Richard's criminal connections," she declared, determination fueling her words. "Find this Razor, see what he knows."

"Agreed," Charlie concurred, unlocking their car. "But we have to be careful, Sarah. We're stepping into dangerous territory."

She knew he was right. But the stakes were high, and she couldn't resist the allure of solving the case. As they drove away, Sarah felt the weight of responsibility settle on her shoulders, heavier than any burden she'd carried before.

•••

"Charlie, look," Sarah whispered, her voice tense. She nodded toward the far end of the parking lot where a shadowy figure lurked, obscured by the dim glow of a flickering streetlight. The figure's eyes seemed to bore into them, unblinking and predatory.

"Damn," Charlie muttered, his grip on the car keys tightening. "Let's move."

They quickened their pace, shoes clicking sharply against the asphalt. Sarah's heart pounded in her chest, adrenaline surging through her veins. The figure remained stationary, watching them intently as they neared the car.

"Stay on your guard, Sarah," Charlie warned, his voice low and steady. "We don't know what we're dealing with here."

"I know," she replied, her breaths coming in short, rapid bursts. Every nerve in her body screamed danger, but she fought to maintain control, her fingers twitching at her side.

The car door swung open with a creak, and Charlie slid behind the wheel, his movements deliberate and practiced. Sarah followed suit, slamming her door shut and locking it in one fluid motion. She couldn't shake the feeling that the shadowy figure had them in its crosshairs.

"Who do you think it is?" Sarah asked, her gaze fixed on the dark silhouette as they pulled away from the curb.

"Could be anyone," Charlie responded, his knuckles white on the steering wheel. "Razor, an old associate of Richard's, or just someone keeping an eye on us."

"Either way, we're being watched," Sarah mused, her brow furrowing in concern. "That means we're getting closer to the truth."

"Or the truth is getting closer to us," Charlie added grimly, navigating the car onto the main road.

Sarah's thoughts raced, her mind a whirlwind of risks and potential dangers. But despite the fear gnawing at her gut, she couldn't deny the thrill that coursed through her. She was in her element, chasing a lead that could crack the case wide open.

"Whatever happens, Charlie," she said, her voice firm with resolve, "we have to see this through."

"Agreed," he replied quietly, his eyes locked on the road ahead.

"But we can't let our guard down, not even for a second."

As they sped into the night, the shadowy figure disappeared from view, swallowed by darkness. But its presence lingered, an ominous specter that threatened to engulf them both.

6

The dimly lit office was cast in an eerie glow by the streetlights outside, shadows creeping along the walls. Sarah's hand hovered over her phone as it buzzed silently on her desk, a number she didn't recognize flashing across the screen.

"Detective Mitchell speaking," she answered, her voice steady despite the tight knot in her stomach. Charlie glanced up from his own desk, sensing the tension in her body language.

"An anonymous tip," the voice on the other end whispered. "Someone knows what happened to Richard Evans."

"Who is this?" Sarah demanded, but the line went dead, leaving her with nothing but a name and an address. She looked at Charlie, who cocked an eyebrow in silent question.

"Anonymous tip," she muttered, scribbling the information down. "Potential witness." Charlie's eyes narrowed, but he nodded.

"Let's check it out, then."

They drove to the address in silence, their thoughts heavy with the weight of the case. The building they pulled up to was rundown, a relic of better times now left to crumble. As they climbed the creaky stairs, Sarah couldn't shake the feeling that they were being watched. She gripped her gun tighter, her knuckles turning white.

"Here it is," Charlie announced, stopping in front of a door with chipped paint. Sarah took a deep breath, trying to quiet her racing thoughts. She knocked, her voice authoritative when the door cracked open.

"Detectives Mitchell and Reynolds. We're here about Richard Evans."

The man who opened the door fully was thin and nervous-looking, his eyes darting between them. "I used to work for him," he stammered, wringing his hands together. "I saw something that night."

"Tell us," Charlie urged, his voice gentle but firm.

"Alex Thompson," the man said shakily, fear etching lines into his face. "I saw them at the pier that night."

Sarah's mind raced, trying to fit this new piece into the puzzle. She needed this case to go right, needed to prove herself. Was Alex Thompson really involved or was someone playing her? Every lead felt like a gamble, and she was tired of losing.

"Can you describe what you saw?" Charlie asked, snapping her back to the present.

"Thompson was arguing with someone," the man continued, swallowing hard. "It looked heated."

"Did you see anyone else? Did Thompson see you?" Sarah pressed, her voice sharp with urgency.

"No, I don't think so. I left as quickly as I could," he whispered, a haunted look in his eyes.

"Thank you," Charlie said, patting the man on the shoulder. "We'll be in touch."

As they made their way back to their car, Sarah couldn't shake the feeling that the walls were closing in around her. The shadows seemed darker, the silence heavier. She glanced back at the building one last time, a shiver running down her spine.

"Is this it, Charlie?" she asked quietly. "Is this the break we've been waiting for?"

"Let's hope so, Sarah," he replied, his voice steady. "But remember, this case is anything but simple. We need to tread carefully."

"Careful" had never been her strong suit, but Sarah nodded in agreement. Desperation gnawed at her, a hunger for the truth she feared she might never find. But she wouldn't give up, not until she unraveled every last thread of Richard Evans' tangled web.

•••

Back at the station, Sarah and Charlie hunched over a table littered with evidence bags, crime scene photos, and hastily scribbled notes. The fluorescent lights buzzed overhead, casting harsh shadows that seemed to echo the darkness of the case itself.

"Let's go over this again," Sarah said, her voice tense. She tapped her pen against the witness statement, her brown eyes narrowed in concentration. "He says he saw Thompson arguing with someone on the pier."

"Right," Charlie replied, rubbing his chin. "And we've got the murder weapon, the blood spatter patterns, and the tire tracks from Thompson's car."

"Something's off," Sarah muttered, her fingers drumming against the table. "Thompson's too smart to leave such obvious clues."

"Unless they wanted us to find them," Charlie suggested, his salt-and-pepper brows furrowing.

"Or someone else is trying to frame Thompson," Sarah countered, her mind racing. She could almost hear the chips falling at a craps table, tempting her with their siren song. But she had a job to do, a mystery to solve.

"Either way, we need to verify this witness's story," Charlie said, pulling out a map of the crime scene. "What do we have on the victim?"

"Evans was shot once in the head, execution-style," Sarah recited, her heart heavy. "No sign of struggle or defensive wounds."

"Dammit, Sarah," Charlie sighed, leaning back in his chair. "What are we missing? There's always something we're not seeing."

"Maybe it's not what we're missing," Sarah whispered, struck by a sudden thought. "What if it's what we're seeing too much of?"

"Explain."

"Look at this photo of the gun," Sarah said, holding up a glossy 8x10. "It's covered in fingerprints. But we know Thompson's too careful for that."

"Right," Charlie agreed, eyes widening as he caught on to her line of thinking.

"Let's compare the prints on this gun with the ones we have on file for Thompson," Sarah suggested, her pulse quickening.

"Good idea," Charlie said, grabbing a fingerprint card from a nearby folder.

Minutes later, they stared at the results in disbelief. The prints on the gun were an exact match for Alex Thompson.

"Someone tampered with our evidence," Sarah breathed, her chest tightening as anger and fear clawed at her insides. "They made it look like Thompson was sloppy."

"Which means someone's playing us," Charlie growled, slamming his fist down on the table. "And they're doing a damn good job of it."

"Whoever it is, they won't win," Sarah vowed, clenching her fists. "We'll find the truth, no matter how deep it's buried."

"Damn right," Charlie agreed, nodding grimly. "Starting now, we leave no stone unturned."

•••

The relentless rain pelted against the windows of Alex Thompson's upscale apartment, casting distorted shadows on the polished hardwood floor. Sarah and Charlie stood in the dimly lit living room, anxiety and determination etched across their faces.

"Thompson," Sarah barked, her voice commanding attention, "you're going to tell us what you know."

Alex Thompson leaned against a sleek black leather couch, piercing blue eyes unwavering as they met her gaze. "I've already told you everything. I didn't kill Richard Evans."

"Your fingerprints were all over the murder weapon," Charlie challenged, his voice thick with suspicion.

"Impossible," Alex replied coolly, folding their arms. "You must be mistaken."

"Someone tampered with our evidence," Sarah hissed, balling her hands into fists. "And we think it was you."

"Me?" Alex's laugh was hollow, devoid of warmth. "Why would I do that? To frame myself?"

"Maybe you wanted to make the investigation messy," Charlie suggested, narrowing his eyes. "Throw us off your trail."

"Or maybe," Alex countered, a sinister smile playing on their lips, "you two are just incompetent."

Sarah bristled at the insult, but reined in her anger. She couldn't afford to let Alex get under her skin. Not now.

"Can we search your place?" Charlie asked, maintaining a level tone despite his partner's agitation.

"Fine." Alex gestured dismissively. "Knock yourselves out."

As they combed through every corner of the apartment, Sarah's mind raced. Her gut screamed that Alex was involved. They had to find something, anything, to prove it.

"Anything?" she whispered to Charlie, the weight of failure settling on her shoulders.

"Nothing concrete," he sighed, rubbing the back of his neck. "This place is clean."

"Too clean," Sarah thought, frustration gnawing at her. But without evidence, they couldn't pin down Alex.

"Alright," Charlie announced, holstering his gun. "We're done here. But this isn't over, Thompson."

"Of course not, detective," Alex replied, smirking. "I look forward to our next little chat."

As Sarah and Charlie left the apartment, the rain seemed to fall even harder than before, as if mirroring their heavy spirits. They had come up empty-handed, but they couldn't let it deter them. The truth was still out there, hidden beneath layers of deception and lies. And they were determined to uncover it, no matter the cost.

•••

Rain splattered against the windshield like bloodstains, casting a melancholy shadow over Sarah's mood. She stared at the list of names in her hand, clenching it tight. It was time to dig deeper and find the truth.

"Let's start with Richard's closest associates," she said, her voice tense with determination.

"Agreed," Charlie replied, pulling up to their first interviewee's residence.

"Mr. Stevens?" Sarah called out as they knocked on the door of a posh suburban home. The door opened, revealing a man in his late 40s wearing an expensive suit and an insincere smile.

"Detectives, what can I do for you?" he asked, ushering them inside.

"Tell us about your relationship with Richard Evans," Charlie began, observing Mr. Stevens' reaction closely.

"Business partners," he responded, his eyes flickering nervously. "Nothing more."

"Did you know Alex Thompson?" Sarah pressed, scrutinizing him for any hint of deceit.

"Thompson? No, never heard of them," he answered, too quickly.

"Interesting," Charlie muttered, making a mental note of the response.

"Alright, thank you for your time," Sarah said, sensing there was nothing more to gain from this encounter.

"Have a good day, detectives," Mr. Stevens replied, his relief palpable as they departed.

"Five interviews down, no one knows anything," Sarah grumbled, frustration building within her. "We're running in circles, Charlie."

"Patience, Sarah," he advised. "The truth will come to light."

Just then, her phone vibrated, signaling an incoming text message. An anonymous tipster claimed that Alex Thompson had been spreading false information about the case, sowing confusion.

"Charlie, we've got something," she said, showing him the text.

"An anonymous source, huh? Could be a trap," he cautioned, his eyebrows furrowed.

"Or it could be the break we need," she countered, her pulse quickening at the prospect of catching Alex in their web of lies. "Either way, we need to follow up on this."

"Alright," Charlie agreed, starting the engine. "But let's proceed with caution."

As they drove towards their next lead, the rain continued to pour, mirroring the storm brewing within Sarah. The truth was out there, waiting to be discovered. And she wouldn't rest until she found it.

•••

A cold gust of wind swept through the dark alley, sending shivers down Sarah's spine as they approached Alex Thompson's residence. The crumbling brick walls and flickering streetlights cast eerie shadows on the damp pavement, creating a sinister atmosphere that mirrored the detectives' determination.

"Ready?" Charlie asked, his voice barely audible over the howling wind.

"Let's do this," Sarah replied, her expression resolute.

They knocked on the door, the sound echoing through the desolate alleyway. After a tense moment, the door creaked open to reveal Alex, their piercing blue eyes betraying no emotion.

"Detectives, what a surprise," Alex said dryly, their calm demeanor unnerving Sarah.

"Cut the crap, Thompson," Sarah snapped, taking a step forward. "We know you've been spreading lies about the investigation."

"Really? And who told you that?" Alex asked, feigning innocence.

"Doesn't matter. We have reason to believe you're trying to derail our investigation," Charlie interjected, his steely gaze locked onto Alex.

"Ridiculous," Alex scoffed, folding their arms. "You're grasping at straws, detectives."

Sarah clenched her fists, her frustration bubbling inside her.

"You expect us to believe it's just a coincidence that false information started circulating right after we questioned you?"

"Maybe someone else is playing games with you," Alex suggested, a hint of a smile playing on their lips. "Or maybe you're just not very good at your jobs."

"Watch it, Thompson," Charlie warned, his patience wearing thin. "We'll be keeping a close eye on you."

"Feel free," Alex replied dismissively, stepping back and closing the door in their faces.

"Dammit!" Sarah exclaimed, kicking the door in anger.

"Easy, Sarah," Charlie consoled her. "We'll get to the bottom of this."

"Something's not right, Charlie," she insisted, her eyes narrowing. "I can feel it."

"Then let's dig deeper," he agreed, nodding towards their car. "Time to start digging into Alex Thompson's past."

As they drove away, Sarah's mind raced with thoughts of unsolved mysteries and hidden connections, fueled by her unwavering dedication to justice. The truth was buried beneath layers of deceit, but she refused to let it stay hidden forever. Deep down, she knew that whatever secrets Alex held would come to light eventually – and when they did, Sarah would be ready.

•••

Rain pattered against the windshield as Sarah and Charlie sat in their unmarked car, parked outside a dimly lit, run-down building that housed the city's archives. The air inside the car was heavy with tension and the scent of stale coffee.

"Got it," Charlie muttered, squinting at the screen of his laptop.

"Previous arrest record for Alex Thompson, five years ago. Breaking and entering, but the charges were dropped."

"Because?" Sarah asked, her brow furrowed.

"Lack of evidence," he replied, frustration evident in his voice. "Seems like our friend has a history of slipping through the cracks."

"Let me see." Sarah grabbed the laptop, scanning the record. Her heart raced, fueled by a mix of anxiety and determination.

"Dammit," she whispered, slamming the laptop shut. "We need concrete evidence, Charlie. Something that'll stick this time."
"Agreed," Charlie said, rubbing his temples. "But we're running out of leads. We need to change our approach."
"Maybe we're missing something," Sarah mused, tapping her fingers on the steering wheel. "Something right under our noses."

"Like what?" Charlie asked, leaning back in his seat.

"Connections," she said, her eyes lighting up. "Whoever tampered with the evidence knew exactly what they were doing. They're either working with Alex or someone with a vested interest in keeping them out of jail."
"Alright," Charlie nodded. "So we look for accomplices or anyone else who might have had a reason to protect Alex."
"Exactly," Sarah affirmed, starting the engine. "No more playing games. Let's bring this bastard down."
As the car pulled away from the curb, Sarah's thoughts swirled around the new angle they would pursue. A knot of determination tightened in her gut, and she vowed that no stone would be left unturned. Whoever was helping Alex Thompson would be exposed, and justice would finally be served.

•••

The rain pelted the windshield of the unmarked police car, each droplet a tiny hammer pounding away at Sarah's nerves. She fidgeted with the worn gambling chip in her pocket – a reminder of her past mistakes and a talisman against future failures.

"Alright," Charlie said, breaking the silence. "We need to reach out to our informants in the criminal underworld. Someone must know something about Alex Thompson."

"Agreed," Sarah replied, her eyes narrowing. "But we need to be discreet. No one can know we're poking around."

"Of course," Charlie nodded. "I'll call Remy. He's always had his ear to the ground."

"Good," Sarah said, gripping the steering wheel until her knuckles turned white. "And I'll reach out to Angie. If anyone knows about Alex's connections, it's her."

"Let's hope they deliver," Charlie muttered, pulling out his phone as Sarah dialed Angie's number.

"Hey, Angie," Sarah said, her voice low and steady. "It's Sarah Mitchell. Listen, we're looking for information on someone – Alex Thompson. Anything you can tell us would be helpful."

"Thompson?" Angie hesitated before continuing. "Yeah, I know them. They're bad news, Sarah. Real slippery. But I'll see what I can find out. Just don't expect any miracles."

"Thanks, Angie," Sarah replied, hanging up the phone. She glanced at Charlie, who was finishing his conversation with Remy.

"Remy said he'd dig around, but no promises," Charlie reported, stuffing his phone back into his pocket.

"Angie said the same," Sarah sighed, her frustration mounting. "We need something solid, Charlie. Something that'll nail Alex to the wall."

"Patience, Sarah," Charlie counseled. "We've chased down leads before. This is just another one."

"Right," she nodded, taking a deep breath to steady herself.

The following day, Sarah's phone buzzed with an incoming call. She snatched it up, her heart racing.

"Sarah, it's Angie," the voice on the other end said. "I've got something for you, but you're not gonna like it. There's a hidden stash of evidence linking Alex Thompson to Richard Evans' murder. But it's in a place that's crawling with danger."

"Where?" Sarah asked, gripping the phone tightly.

"An abandoned warehouse down by the docks," Angie replied. "But be careful, Sarah. The people guarding it aren't the type to mess around."

"Thanks, Angie," Sarah said, her voice wavering slightly. "We owe you one."

"Damn right you do," Angie retorted. "Now go get that bastard."

"Will do," Sarah promised, disconnecting the call and turning to Charlie. "Angie came through. We've got a lead."

"Let's hope it's the one we need," Charlie replied, his eyes determined. "Time to bring Alex Thompson to justice."

As they drove toward the warehouse, Sarah's pulse quickened, her thoughts a whirlwind of fear and anticipation. The chip in her pocket seemed to burn against her skin, a constant reminder that this time, she couldn't afford to lose.

•••

Sarah's heart pounded as they approached Alex Thompson's residence, the newfound evidence weighing heavy in her hand.

The sun dipped below the horizon, casting menacing shadows across the street. Charlie parked their unmarked car a block away, and they walked the rest of the distance, anticipation building with every step.

"Are you ready for this?" Charlie asked, his voice low and determined.

"More than ever," Sarah replied, clutching the incriminating photos and documents tight against her chest.

They reached Alex's front door, the dim porch light casting an eerie glow over the scene. Sarah knocked forcefully, her knuckles rapping against the solid wood. Moments later, the door swung open, revealing Alex Thompson, their piercing blue eyes cold and calculating.

"Detectives," Alex said, feigning surprise. "What a pleasure."

"Cut the crap, Alex," Sarah spat, her anger bubbling to the surface. "We've got you dead to rights."

"Really?" Alex replied, raising an eyebrow. "And what makes you so sure?"

Charlie pulled out the damning photos and shoved them at Alex.

"These. Taken from your secret stash. You're linked to Richard Evans' murder."

"Is that so?" Alex said, their voice dripping with disdain. "You two have been busy, haven't you?"

"Admit it, Alex," Sarah growled, her hands shaking with adrenaline. "You killed Richard Evans. And we can prove it."

"Alright," Alex sighed, their icy façade finally cracking. "I did it. But you'll never understand why."

"Try us," Charlie demanded, his eyes locked on Alex.

"Richard was going to expose my criminal operations," Alex confessed, their voice barely above a whisper. "He couldn't be allowed to live."

"Nothing justifies murder, Alex," Sarah said, her voice laced with disgust.

"Maybe not," Alex replied, their eyes dark and hollow. "But you don't know the half of it."

"Doesn't matter," Charlie cut in. "You're going down, Alex. You can't escape justice this time." Alex's gaze fell to the floor, resignation etched across their face. "I guess I always knew it would catch up with me eventually."

"Damn right," Sarah muttered, pulling out her handcuffs. "Alex Thompson, you're under arrest for the murder of Richard Evans."

As she snapped the cold metal around Alex's wrists, Sarah felt a surge of satisfaction. The long nights, the dangerous encounters, the constant frustration - it had all led to this moment. They had finally cornered the cunning adversary that had haunted their investigation from the start.

"Let's go," Charlie ordered, guiding Alex towards the car. "It's over."

"Is it ever really over, Detective?" Alex asked, their voice tinged with bitterness.

"Maybe not," Sarah admitted, her eyes locked on the defeated figure before her. "But at least we've put an end to your reign of terror."

7

The rain pelted against the windshield, a relentless symphony punctuated by the thrum of the wiper blades. Sarah's knuckles turned white as she gripped the steering wheel, her focus split between the treacherous road and the gnawing thoughts that ate away at her insides. Charlie sat beside her in the passenger seat, his gaze locked on the screen of his phone.

"Read it again," Sarah murmured, her voice barely audible above the din of the storm.

"Sarah, you've heard it already," Charlie replied, concern etched into the lines of his face.

"Please," she insisted, her breath hitching with the weight of her anxiety.

"Alright." Charlie cleared his throat. "'This is your only warning, detectives. Back off the Thompson case, or you'll wish you had. This is not an empty threat.'"

"Any idea who sent it?" she asked, already knowing the answer.

"None. It's untraceable."

Sarah's heart raced, her mind spinning with paranoia. The sight of a car approaching in the rearview mirror made her flinch, every nerve on high alert. She forced herself to breathe, to stay grounded in the present moment despite the whirlwind of fear threatening to consume her.

"Charlie," she began, her voice shaking, "what if they go after my family? Or yours?"

"Sarah, we're going to keep everyone safe. We've dealt with threats before," he reassured her, placing a comforting hand on her arm.

"Y-yeah, but this feels different. Like they know our weaknesses, our secrets." She swallowed hard, her grip tightening on the wheel. "I'm just scared, Charlie. You're like family to me, and I can't lose anyone else."

"Hey," he said softly, turning to face her fully. "We're in this together, alright? We'll watch each other's backs. And we won't back down, not until we bring Thompson to justice."

"Promise?" she asked, her eyes filled with a vulnerability she rarely showed.

"Promise," he replied, his tone resolute and unyielding.

The rain continued its torrential assault on the car, but for a brief moment, Sarah found solace in Charlie's words. She knew the storm inside her wouldn't subside completely — not until they closed this case — but as long as they faced it together, she could weather whatever came their way.

•••

A cacophony of barking greeted Sarah as she approached Emma's small, yellow house. Leaves crunched beneath her boots, the autumn chill nipping at her exposed skin.

"Emma, it's me," Sarah called out, trying to keep her voice steady. The door creaked open, revealing her sister in a faded college sweatshirt, her dark hair pulled back into a messy bun.

"Sarah? What are you doing here?" Emma asked, her eyes widening with surprise.

"Can we talk inside?" She shifted her weight uneasily, scanning the quiet street.

"Sure, come on in." Emma stepped aside, allowing Sarah to enter the cozy living room filled with mismatched furniture and framed family photos — memories of better days.

"Emma, I need you to listen carefully," Sarah began, her heart pounding in her chest. "You could be in danger."

"Danger?" Emma's brows furrowed, concern etched on her face. "What do you mean?"

"Someone threatened Charlie and me. They want us off our current case." She hesitated, swallowing hard. "They know about our past, Em, and they might target you."

"Jesus, Sarah." Emma sank down onto the worn couch, her hands trembling. "What can I do?"

"Stay vigilant. Keep your doors locked, don't walk alone at night, and if you see anything suspicious, call me immediately."

"Okay, okay. I'll be careful, I promise." Emma nodded vigorously, her eyes brimming with fear.

"Thank you," Sarah whispered, hugging her sister tightly. The scent of lavender shampoo brought a rush of nostalgia, a bittersweet reminder of their shared childhood.

As Sarah stepped back outside, Charlie's voice buzzed through her earpiece. "Sarah, I've been thinking – maybe we should relocate our loved ones while we're working this case."

"Relocate? To where?" She glanced around, the autumn breeze rustling the dry leaves.

"Safe houses. Temporary, of course, but it'll give us peace of mind until we take down Thompson and his operation." The determination in Charlie's voice was palpable.

Sarah considered the idea, weighing the risks against the potential benefits. "Alright," she finally agreed, her resolve hardening. "Let's do it."

"Good. I'll make the arrangements." Charlie's voice held a note of relief as the line went dead.

Sarah took one last look at her sister's house, her chest tightening with the weight of responsibility. She knew that Emma's safety, along with everyone else's, rested on her shoulders – and she wouldn't let them down, no matter the cost.

•••

The neon lights of the casino beckoned like a siren's call, their seductive glow casting long shadows on the pavement. Sarah stood outside, her hand gripping the door handle, knuckles white with tension. She closed her eyes, desperately trying to ward off the urge that threatened to consume her.

"Sarah, what are you doing here?" Charlie's voice came through the earpiece, sharp with concern.
"Nothing," she lied, her breaths shallow and uneven. "Just needed some air."
"Sarah, I know that's not true. Don't do this." The worry in Charlie's voice was palpable.
"Okay, fine," she admitted, her grip on the door handle slackening. "I'm at the casino. But I haven't gone in. Not yet."
"Gambling isn't going to help anyone, especially not now," Charlie reminded her gently. "We need you at your best for this case."

"I know, I know," she whispered, her heart pounding in her chest. "But the urge is so strong, Charlie. It's like I can feel the dice in my hands, hear the roulette wheel spinning…"

"Remember why we're doing this, Sarah," Charlie implored. "Think about Emma. Think about all the people counting on us to bring Thompson down."

Sarah clenched her fists, her nails digging into her palms as images of Emma's frightened face flashed through her mind. She knew that giving in to her addiction would only make matters worse, but the temptation gnawed at her relentlessly. "Charlie, I..." Her voice wavered, betraying the vulnerability she'd been hiding. "I'm scared. I've never been this close to losing it all before."

"Hey," Charlie said softly, his tone shifting from concern to comfort. "You're not alone in this. I'm here for you. We'll get through this together, okay?"

"Okay," Sarah agreed, her voice barely audible.

"Promise me you'll walk away from that casino right now," Charlie urged.

"I promise." The words felt heavy on her tongue, but she knew she had to say them. With one last glance at the enticing glow of the neon lights, Sarah turned and walked away, her resolve stronger than ever before.

•••

The sun dipped below the horizon, casting long shadows across the small, cluttered office. Sarah sat at her desk, hunched over a myriad of case files and photographs spread out before her. The dim light from the desk lamp flickered, casting eerie shadows on the walls. She wiped her tired eyes, trying to refocus.

"Sarah," Charlie said, sliding into the seat across from her. "We need to devise a new plan – our current approach isn't getting us anywhere."

"Agreed." Sarah's voice was hoarse, exhaustion lacing every word. "But where do we start?"

"Thompson's criminal network is vast," Charlie mused, tapping his fingers on the desk. "But we know they can't operate without their lieutenants. If we can find a way to infiltrate their ranks, gather enough evidence against them..."

"Then we weaken Thompson's position," Sarah finished, sitting up straighter. A glimmer of hope sparked within her.

"Exactly," Charlie confirmed. "We'll have to play this smart — one wrong move could cost us everything."

"Let's start by identifying their key players," Sarah suggested, rifling through the case files. "If we can establish a pattern in their operations, maybe we can exploit a weakness."

"Good idea." Charlie nodded, pulling a stack of files towards him. "We should also look for any disgruntled insiders who might be willing to talk."

"Right." Sarah sighed, rubbing her temples. The pressure of the investigation weighed heavily on her, but she couldn't let it break her. Emma's safety hung in the balance, and she'd be damned if she let anything happen to her sister.

"Sarah," Charlie said gently, noticing her distress. "Don't forget you're not alone in this. We're a team. We'll bring Thompson down. Together."

"Thank you, Charlie," Sarah whispered, her voice cracking. "I just... I can't let them hurt my family."

"Then we won't," Charlie said with conviction. "We'll do whatever it takes to protect them."

"I know." Sarah took a deep breath, her resolve hardening. "Let's get to work."

For hours, they scoured the files, piecing together fragments of information in hopes of uncovering a weakness in Thompson's criminal empire. Each lead, each connection fueled Sarah's determination to bring justice to those affected by Alex Thompson's reign of terror.

"Hey, look at this," Charlie said, pointing to a photograph of a known associate. "This guy has been seen with several of Thompson's lieutenants."

"Interesting," Sarah replied, studying the image. "He could be our way in."

"Let's hope so," Charlie agreed. "We're running out of time."

"Then let's make every second count," Sarah declared. And as the night wore on, their plan began to take shape – a meticulous blueprint designed to dismantle Alex Thompson's world, brick by brick.

•••

The rain pelted against the windowpanes, and a gust of wind sent shivers through the cramped office. Sarah sat hunched over her desk, her eyes bloodshot and heavy as she poured over the evidence before her.

"Sarah, when was the last time you slept?" Charlie asked, his concern evident in the deep furrows that creased his brow.

"Sleep is for the weak," she muttered, rubbing her temples as if trying to massage away the exhaustion. "We're close, Charlie. I can feel it."

"Alright, alright," he conceded, pulling up a chair beside her. "So, what do we have?"

"Connections," Sarah replied, tapping on a map covered in red strings and pushpins. "But they're slippery. Every time we think we've got something solid, it evaporates."

"Like a ghost," Charlie mused, staring at the web of crime they were trying to unravel. "But ghosts always leave traces."

"Exactly," Sarah said, her heart racing with adrenaline-fueled determination. She gestured towards a series of photographs pinned to the wall. "These people are our key – if we can find out how they fit into Thompson's organization, we can start to dismantle it."

"Right," Charlie agreed, scanning the faces before them. "Let's get to work."

They dove headfirst into the investigation, piecing together bits of intel that began to form a clearer picture of the criminal network. As the hours ticked by, the shadows grew long and their eyelids felt heavier, but they refused to stop.

"Charlie, look at this," Sarah whispered, her voice hoarse from exhaustion as she pointed to a blurry image of a man meeting with one of Thompson's known associates. "This could be our break."

"Good catch," he said, leaning in for a closer look. "Let's follow this lead. If he's a weak link, we might be able to use it to our advantage."

"Let's go," Sarah said, her legs trembling as she rose from her seat. She knew that pushing herself to the brink of collapse was dangerous, but the thought of Thompson slipping through their fingers fueled her resolve.

As they ventured out into the rain-soaked night, Sarah couldn't help but feel the weight of the world bearing down on her shoulders. Every shadow held a potential threat, every passerby an enemy in disguise. The paranoia gnawed at her like a relentless beast, threatening to devour her sanity.

"Sarah," Charlie whispered, placing a reassuring hand on her arm as they approached the meeting location. "We've got this. No matter how tired or scared we are, we can't let them win."

"Right," Sarah agreed, swallowing the lump in her throat. "I'm not going to let my family suffer because I couldn't stay strong enough to see this through."

"Exactly," Charlie affirmed, his voice steady and unwavering. "Now let's go get some justice."

Together, they pressed forward, following the trail that would lead them one step closer to unmasking the man behind the curtain – Alex Thompson. And with each passing moment, Sarah's determination only grew, fueled by the love for her family and the burning desire to see justice prevail.

•••

The sun had set, casting long shadows across the room as Sarah walked through the door. The dim light of a single lamp illuminated her desk, where a brown package lay unopened. It was addressed to her, with no return address or any indication of who it was from.

"Another day, another lead," she muttered, slumping into her chair and tearing open the package. As she pulled out its contents, her heart caught in her throat.

"Jesus Christ," she whispered, staring at the compromising photos of her sister, Emma, that were spread across her desk. Each photo seemed more invasive than the last, showcasing intimate moments captured without consent. Along with the images, there was a folded piece of paper, and Sarah's hands shook as she unfolded it.

"Back off, Mitchell, or your sister's life will be hell," the note read, clearly written by Alex Thompson. "This is just the beginning."

"Sarah? What's wrong?" Charlie asked, concern evident in his voice as he entered the room.

"Thompson," she said, gritting her teeth. "He's got my sister, Charlie. Photos of her... He's threatening her if we don't back off the case."

"Damn it," Charlie muttered, his face contorting with anger. "We need to act fast before he escalates."

"Escalates?" Sarah snapped, her desperation mounting. "How much worse can it get? He's already invaded her privacy! Threatened her life!"

"Sarah, I know you're scared," Charlie said, his tone gentle but firm. "But we have to keep our heads. This means we're getting closer, and he's feeling the pressure."

"Pressure?" Sarah scoffed. "I'm the one under pressure, Charlie. My family, my friends, everyone around me – they're all potential targets now!"

"Then let's use that pressure, Sarah," Charlie insisted. "Let it fuel us to bring him down."

"Fuel?" she repeated, her voice cracking as tears welled in her eyes. "Charlie, I'm exhausted. I can't sleep, I can barely eat... and now this? How am I supposed to keep going?"

"Because you're strong, Sarah," Charlie said, his voice unwavering. "You've always been strong. And we'll get through this together."

"Strong," Sarah whispered, wiping away the tears that threatened to fall. As much as she wanted to break down, she knew Charlie was right – they had to keep moving forward.

"Okay," she said, taking a deep breath. "We'll keep going. But we need to act fast. He's getting desperate, and there's no telling what he'll do next."

"Agreed," Charlie nodded. "We'll track him down, Sarah. I promise you that."

With renewed determination, Sarah and Charlie gathered the evidence and prepared for the long night ahead. The road to justice would be difficult and treacherous, but their resolve was unbreakable. Together, they would face the darkness and bring Alex Thompson to his knees.

•••

Sarah stood at the window, her breath fogging up the glass as she gazed out into the dark night. The city's neon lights blurred in the distance, casting eerie shadows on the pavement below. Her heart pounded like a jackhammer, a relentless reminder of the stakes at hand.

"Charlie," she said, her voice tight with determination. "We need to confront Alex Thompson directly. It's the only way to end this."

"Are you sure?" Charlie asked, concern etched on his face. "That's risky, Sarah. We don't know what we're walking into."

"Exactly," she replied, eyes locked onto the horizon. "But we can't wait any longer. He won't stop until he destroys everything I care about."

"Alright," Charlie sighed, the weight of their decision settling on his shoulders. "Let's do it."

Sarah turned to face him, her resolve strengthening with each beat of her heart. "We'll bring justice to the victims and put an end to Thompson's reign."

As they gathered their weapons and prepared for the confrontation, Sarah felt adrenaline surge through her veins, igniting her senses. She tightened her grip on her pistol, its cold metal grounding her in the moment.

"Remember," Charlie warned, checking the chamber of his gun, "stick together, no matter what."

"Of course," Sarah nodded, her focus razor-sharp. "We've come too far to let anything tear us apart now."

They slipped out into the night, the air heavy with tension and anticipation. Each step echoed against the concrete, punctuating their thoughts with the pulsating rhythm of danger.

"Sarah," Charlie whispered, his breath clouding in the cold air, "you ready for this?"

"More than ever," she replied, her voice steady despite the storm raging within her. "I owe it to the victims... and to myself."

They approached Alex Thompson's lair, the dim light of an old streetlamp casting their shadows on the crumbling brick walls. As they neared the entrance, Sarah's heart hammered in her chest, a cacophony of fear, rage, and determination.

"Whatever happens," she thought, steeling herself for the final showdown, "I'll fight to the end."

•••

The pier loomed ahead, its wooden boards creaking under the weight of their footsteps. The moon cast a ghostly glow on the water below, as if whispering a warning in the stillness. Sarah's pulse raced, her senses heightened, and she tried to steady her breathing.

"Everyone's here," Charlie said, his voice low and cautious.

Their allies – trusted friends and colleagues – emerged from the shadows, nodding grimly.

"Remember the plan," Sarah instructed, her voice taut with determination. "Surround him, but don't engage until Charlie and I give the signal."

"Got it," responded Officer Daniels, his fingers twitching nervously on the grip of his gun. A bead of sweat rolled down his face, glistening in the moonlight.

"Stay sharp," added Detective Ramirez, her dark eyes scanning the surroundings for any sign of danger. She adjusted the Kevlar vest beneath her jacket, the movement betraying her own anxiety.

"Where do you think he is?" whispered Officer Jenkins, his eyes darting between the abandoned warehouses and empty fishing boats that lined the pier.

"Patience," Sarah murmured, her gaze fixed on the darkness enveloping their target. She could feel Alex Thompson's presence like a malignant shadow, taunting them with every passing moment.

"Sarah," Charlie touched her arm gently, pulling her from her thoughts. "You've got this. We all have your back."

"Thank you," she managed a tight smile, grateful for his unwavering support. But deep within her, doubt gnawed at her resolve like a ravenous beast – would they really be able to catch Thompson? Could she protect everyone?

"Watch the entrances," she ordered, her voice cutting through the silence. "He won't leave without a fight."

"Copy that," replied Officer Daniels, his jaw set in determination.

"Let's do this," Detective Ramirez said, her voice steely.

"Ready when you are," Charlie affirmed, his hand resting on the grip of his gun. He met Sarah's gaze, a silent promise exchanged between them.

Sarah inhaled deeply, the ocean air filling her lungs with resolve. The time had come to face Alex Thompson – and she would not back down.

8

The phone rang, jolting Sarah awake from her restless sleep. Her eyes snapped open to the darkness of her apartment, heart pounding in her chest. She fumbled for the source of the noise, snatching up the cell from the bedside table.

"Sarah Mitchell," she answered, voice cracking with lingering exhaustion.

"Got something you need to see." The voice on the other end was gruff, distorted. Anonymous.

"Who is this?" she demanded.

"Doesn't matter. Warehouse on Dock Street. Midnight."

Click. The line went dead.

"Dammit," Sarah muttered under her breath, tossing the phone back onto the bed. She rubbed her temples, trying to shake off the remnants of sleep. Was this a genuine tip or just another wild goose chase? She glanced at the clock: 11:15 PM. Only one way to find out.

"Charlie, meet me at the warehouse on Dock Street. Got an anonymous tip," she texted her partner as she hastily pulled on her boots and jacket.

"Be there in ten," came the almost immediate response.

The night air was cold, biting at her cheeks as she stepped outside, but she barely felt it. Adrenaline pumped through her veins, propelling her forward, driven by the possibility that this could be the break they needed.

Sarah arrived at the warehouse first, casting her flashlight around the darkened building, searching for any signs of life.

Charlie's car rolled up moments later, headlights slicing through the darkness like a knife.

"Evening, partner," he greeted, stepping out of his vehicle. "What have we got?"

"Anonymous tip," she replied, nodding towards the warehouse. "Said there's something going on here."

"Let's take a look then."

Together, they approached the warehouse, senses heightened. The door creaked as Sarah pushed it open, revealing a dimly lit space filled with crates and boxes. They moved cautiously, their flashlights casting eerie shadows on the walls.

"Damn," Charlie whispered as they rounded a corner. "Look at this."

Stacked high against the wall were bags of white powder, each marked with a different symbol. Drugs. And not just a small-time operation, either; this was big.

"Keep looking," Sarah urged, her mind racing. Who in town was involved? How deep did this go?

As they continued their search, they came across ledgers filled with names and numbers, scrawled handwriting that hinted at a complex network of dealers and customers. Photos of familiar faces stared back at them from the pages, sending chills down their spines.

"Can't believe it," Charlie muttered, shaking his head. "Half the town's caught up in this."

"Let's gather everything we can find," Sarah said, already snapping pictures of the evidence with her phone. "We need to connect the dots, figure out who's behind all this."

They worked methodically, cataloging the evidence spread before them. With each new discovery, the web of deceit grew larger, extending its tendrils throughout the town like a cancer.

"Charlie," Sarah murmured as they regrouped, her voice low and heavy with the weight of their findings. "We've got our work cut out for us."

"Damn right we do," he agreed, eyes steely with resolve. "But we'll bring 'em down. You and me, partner."

And as they stood there amongst the darkness and the secrets, Sarah knew they would. Together, they would tear down the criminal empire that threatened their town, one piece at a time.

•••

The smell of stale cigarettes and fear filled the cramped, dimly lit room as Sarah and Charlie cornered their suspect. Sweat dripped down the man's unshaven face, his eyes darting between the two detectives as if searching for an escape.

"Start talking," Sarah demanded, her voice sharp as a knife. "Who's running this operation?"

"Alright, alright," the man stammered, clearly weighing his options. "I don't know his real name – we just call him 'The Boss.' He's like a ghost, barely shows his face."

"Hard to believe," Charlie scoffed, stepping closer, looming over the trembling man. "Someone's gotta be calling the shots."

"Look, I swear that's all I know!" the suspect insisted, desperation seeping into his voice. "He's got lieutenants and all that, but he stays in the shadows."

Sarah studied the man's expression, searching for any trace of deceit. Could he really be telling the truth? She glanced at Charlie, who nodded in silent agreement.

"Tell us about these lieutenants," she pressed, unwilling to let up.

"Fine," the man sighed, defeated. "There's four main ones. They handle different parts of the operation – drugs, money, enforcement, and recruitment. They're all bad news, trust me."

"Names," Charlie growled, impatience simmering beneath the surface. "Give us names."

"Okay, okay," the suspect conceded, rattling off a list of aliases. "But that's all I've got, I swear!"

"Every little bit helps," Sarah reassured him, her mind racing with the new information.

As they left the room, Charlie turned to her, concern etched onto his face. "This is bigger than we thought, isn't it?"

"Definitely," she replied, feeling the weight of the case on her shoulders. "This isn't just some small-town operation. It's connected to something much larger."

"Which means we need to tread carefully," Charlie warned, his voice heavy with experience. "We're not just dealing with local thugs anymore."

"Whatever it takes," Sarah vowed, a fierce determination burning in her eyes. "We'll bring them all down – from The Boss to the lowest recruit."

"Right," Charlie agreed, his resolve matching hers. "Together, partner."

•••

The sterile light of the station's break room flickered above Sarah and Charlie as they hunched over a worn-out map, plotting their infiltration. It was time to go undercover.

"Remind me again why we're doing this?" Sarah asked, her fingers tracing the grid-like pattern of streets.

"Because," Charlie replied, his gaze fixed on the map, "we need to get inside this operation and gather enough evidence to bring them all down."

"Right," she nodded, her mind whirring with thoughts of the looming risks. "You know I've got your back, Charlie."

"Always," he said, offering her a reassuring smile.

Their plan hinged on posing as low-level recruits. It wasn't ideal, but given the lieutenants' aliases they'd uncovered, it was their best shot at blending in. They had to be careful – one misstep could blow their cover.

"Let's review our roles," Sarah suggested, her voice steady and focused. "I'll pose as a courier, while you handle money laundering. We need to get close to each lieutenant without arousing suspicion."

"Sounds like a plan," Charlie agreed.

"Okay, let's prep for tomorrow," Sarah said, determination sparking in her eyes. "We need to look the part."

They spent the next few hours gathering the necessary resources: burner phones, cash for bribes, weapons concealed beneath civilian clothes, and fake IDs that would pass muster with even the most discerning criminal. Every piece of equipment was meticulously chosen, designed to keep them alive and undetected.

"Think this'll work?" Charlie asked, studying their new personas in the mirror.

"Only one way to find out," Sarah replied, her reflection staring back with steely resolve.

As she tucked a slim blade into her boot, Sarah couldn't help but feel a twinge of doubt. Risking their lives to infiltrate a dangerous criminal operation was a gamble, but she'd never been one for playing it safe. The stakes were high, and the odds against them, but Sarah Mitchell didn't back down from a challenge.

"Remember," Charlie reminded her, his voice firm but gentle, "we're in this together."

"Always," she echoed, meeting his gaze in the mirror. And with that, they set off into the night, ready to face whatever the underworld had in store for them.

•••

The deafening bass from the underground club reverberated through Sarah's chest, as she and Charlie stood at the entrance, their eyes adjusting to the dim lighting. They'd spent weeks establishing their aliases as low-level criminals, earning enough trust to be invited to this secret meeting of the operation's lieutenants.

"Damn," Charlie muttered, his voice barely audible over the pounding music. "Risky business."

"Stay sharp," Sarah replied, scanning the room for familiar faces from their investigation.

As they wove through the crowd, Sarah felt a hand on her shoulder. She turned to see Marco, one of the men they'd identified as a key player in the operation. Her heart raced, but she kept her face neutral.

"Nice work on that job last week," he said, leaning close to make himself heard. "Boss is impressed."

"Thanks," Sarah replied, forcing a tight smile. "Just doing what I can."

"Keep it up," Marco grinned, before disappearing back into the throng.

"Too close," Charlie whispered, his eyes wide.

"Get used to it," Sarah shot back, steeling herself for the challenges ahead.

They eventually found themselves in a cordoned-off area, where the leaders of the criminal operation were gathered around a table cluttered with maps, cash, and weapons. As the discussion began, Sarah focused on absorbing every detail she could – names, locations, upcoming deals – while Charlie subtly snapped photos with a hidden camera.

"Need more product," snarled a man they knew only as Viper. "Demand's high."

"Already on it," another lieutenant assured him. "Got a shipment coming in next week."

"Better not screw this up, Eddie," Viper warned, his gaze piercing. "Or you'll answer to me."

"Understood," Eddie nodded, beads of sweat on his brow.

"Good," Viper said, turning to the assembled group. "Now let's get back to work."

As the meeting dispersed, Sarah and Charlie slipped away, their minds racing with the information they'd gathered.

"Did you get everything?" she asked, her voice barely a whisper.

"Think so," Charlie confirmed, his eyes darting around for potential eavesdroppers.

"Let's go before our luck runs out," Sarah urged, the weight of their deception heavy on her shoulders.

"Agreed," Charlie nodded, and together, they made their way back through the pulsing crowd, their hearts pounding in time with the relentless beat.

•••

The sun dipped below the horizon, casting an orange glow over the quiet town. Sarah's heart raced as she and Charlie observed a nondescript warehouse from a safe distance, clad in dark clothing to blend in with the shadows. She could feel the adrenaline pumping through her veins, feeding her determination.

"Ready?" Charlie asked, his voice low.

"Let's do this," Sarah replied, gripping the binoculars tightly.

They crept closer, relying on their stealth and quick wits. Through the binoculars, Sarah watched figures moving in and out of the warehouse, exchanging large bags and boxes. The operation was larger than they'd anticipated.

"Drugs," Charlie whispered, noting the telltale signs of narcotics trafficking.

"Money laundering too," Sarah added, spotting stacks of cash being loaded onto a truck.

"Got names?" Charlie questioned.

"Viper's running the show. Eddie's his right-hand man."

"Any others?"

"Working on it," Sarah muttered, her eyes scanning the scene for more faces.

"Careful, love. Push too hard and you'll break."

"Can't afford not to push," she retorted, the weight of their mission heavy on her mind.

"Fair enough."

Sarah focused on the key players, memorizing each face and mannerism. Viper, a man with a snake tattoo slithering up his neck; Eddie, his eyes darting nervously back and forth; a woman called Ruby, her red hair unmistakable even in the dim light; and Gideon, a hulking brute with a cruel smile.

"Got 'em," she announced, lowering the binoculars.

"Good work," Charlie praised, snapping photos of each suspect.

"Let's get out of here before we're spotted," Sarah suggested, feeling the pressure mounting.

"Agreed."

As they retreated, Sarah couldn't shake the nagging feeling that this case was personal. The stakes were higher than ever, and she had no intention of letting the criminals win.

"Charlie," she whispered urgently, "we have to bring them down. No matter what."

"Of course," he replied, his eyes reflecting the fire in hers.

"We'll get 'em, Sarah. We always do."

"Damn right we will," she vowed, her resolve unwavering as they disappeared into the night.

•••

Sarah's phone buzzed on the nightstand, jolting her awake. She squinted at the screen, a sinking feeling settling in her chest as she registered the single word: COMPROMISED.

"Charlie," she whispered urgently, shaking him awake. "It's our informant."

"Wha'?" he mumbled, eyes still closed.

"Dead. Found 'em in an alley."

"Shit." He sat up, rubbing his face wearily. "We need to act fast."

"Agreed."

They dressed quickly, heading out into the cold night air, their breaths visible with each exhale.

"Who did this?" Sarah demanded, her heart pounding as they approached the crime scene.

"Viper's crew, most likely," Charlie replied grimly. "Our informant was getting too close."

"Damn it!" Sarah slammed her fist against a nearby wall, frustration and guilt coursing through her veins.

"Hey, hey, love," Charlie said, placing a calming hand on her shoulder. "This isn't your fault."

"Feels like it," she muttered, staring down at the lifeless body of their informant, blood pooling around them.

"Listen," he continued, his voice steady, "we can't let their death be in vain. We have to shut this operation down. Now."

"Before it spreads any further," she agreed, her resolve hardening.

"Exactly."

"How do we move forward?" she asked, her mind racing with possibilities and potential pitfalls.

"Keep gathering intel," Charlie suggested. "Push harder, smarter. But remember—"

"Be cautious. I know, I know."

"Good."

As they stood over the body, Sarah couldn't help but feel a renewed sense of urgency. This wasn't just another case; this was a fight for justice, and she refused to let anyone else die on her watch.

"Let's get to work," she said, her voice determined and unwavering. "No more playing it safe."

"Agreed," Charlie nodded, his eyes meeting hers in a silent promise.

"Viper won't know what hit him."

•••

Charlie's hands gripped the steering wheel as Sarah stared at the looming warehouse, her eyes scanning for signs of movement. This was it—the final showdown. They parked a block away, ready to gather their allies.

"Remember," Sarah said, tapping each face on the screen of her phone, "these people are putting their lives on the line for us."

"Got it," Charlie replied, adding his own contacts to the list. "We'll make sure they're safe."

"Good." She hit send and waited for their team to assemble.

Within minutes, unmarked cars pulled up, and familiar faces emerged from the shadows—off-duty officers, ex-military, even a few vigilantes—all sharing a common goal: justice.

"Alright, listen up!" Charlie barked, commanding attention. "Our intel says Viper is inside, along with his top lieutenants. They know we're coming, so expect heavy resistance."

"Stay sharp," Sarah added, her voice firm. "And watch each other's backs."

Their makeshift army nodded, determination etched on every face.

"Let's move out," Charlie ordered.

As one, they advanced toward the warehouse, weapons at the ready. Sarah could feel her heart pounding in her chest, adrenaline surging through her veins. *This ends tonight*, she vowed.

"Breaching in three... two... one..." Charlie counted down, then kicked open the door.

Gunfire erupted from within, a hailstorm of bullets that sent them diving for cover. Gritting her teeth, Sarah fired back, her aim steady and true.

"Go, go, go!" Charlie shouted, leading the charge as they stormed the building.

"Take the high ground!" Sarah ordered, pointing to a catwalk above. A few officers scrambled upward, securing a vantage point.

Think ahead, stay focused, she reminded herself, weaving between crates and gunfire. She spotted Viper's thugs, taking them down with precision shots.

"Sarah! Charlie!" a voice called out above the chaos. "We found a locked door—might be Viper's office!"

"Cover us!" Sarah yelled back, sprinting toward the door with Charlie at her side. She could feel sweat stinging her eyes, but she wouldn't let it slow her down.

"Stand back," Charlie warned, aiming his gun at the lock. The door burst open, revealing a dimly lit room and their ultimate target.

"Viper," Sarah growled, leveling her weapon at the smirking crime lord.

"Detectives," he sneered, not even reaching for his own gun. "Took you long enough."

"Drop the act," Charlie demanded. "You're under arrest."

"Am I?" Viper taunted. "Or is this just another one of your gambles, Detective Mitchell?"

"Shut up!" Sarah snapped, feeling her heart race, her fingers twitching on the trigger.

"Sarah, don't let him—" Charlie warned.

"Too late," she said softly, then fired.

Viper crumpled to the floor, gasping in pain. His empire shattered before him, he finally knew defeat.

"Good shot," Charlie murmured, cuffing the wounded criminal.

"Thanks." Sarah exhaled, relief flooding her system. The gamble had paid off.

•••

The warehouse echoed with the sound of handcuffs clicking shut, as Sarah and Charlie watched their allies secure the remaining members of Viper's gang. The air was thick with tension, the stench of gunpowder and sweat lingering as a reminder of the violent confrontation that had just unfolded.

"Finally," Charlie muttered, wiping sweat off his brow, his relief palpable. "It's done."

"Is it?" Sarah asked, her gaze fixed on Viper, now cuffed and writhing in pain on the floor. "We still need to make sure this doesn't happen again."

"Sarah," Charlie placed a reassuring hand on her shoulder. "We've won. This town will be safe now. Let's focus on that."

"Alright, let's get them out of here," Sarah instructed her fellow officers, her voice steady despite the adrenaline still coursing through her veins.

"Detective Mitchell, Detective Reynolds," one of the officers called out, approaching them with a sense of urgency. "We found something you should see."

"Lead the way," Charlie said, exchanging glances with Sarah.

They followed the officer into a back room, its walls lined with shelves filled with firearms, drugs, and stacks of cash. It was the evidence they needed to ensure justice would be served and the criminal operation dismantled.

"Looks like our work here is done," Charlie remarked, his eyes scanning the room with a mixture of disgust and satisfaction.

"Work's never done, Charlie," Sarah replied, her mind already racing ahead to the next challenge. "But for now, we've made a difference."

"Damn right we did," he agreed, clapping her on the back as they surveyed the room.

"Charlie," she said, suddenly serious. "Thank you, for everything."

"Hey, what are partners for?" he smiled warmly. "Now, let's get these bastards to the station and call it a night."

"Sounds like a plan," Sarah grinned, feeling a weight lift from her shoulders as they began gathering the evidence. For once, the odds had been in her favor, and she couldn't help but savor the victory.

Together, Sarah and Charlie led the criminals out of the warehouse and into the waiting police vehicles. The flashing red and blue lights cut through the darkness, signaling an end to the criminal reign that had gripped their town.

As they drove away, Sarah turned to Charlie, a smile playing on her lips. "You think we'll ever get used to this?"

"Never," he replied with a grin. "And I wouldn't have it any other way."

9

The low hum of the laptop fan filled the dimly-lit motel room, accompanied by the sporadic tapping of keys. Sarah's fingers danced across the keyboard as she navigated through a maze of digital breadcrumbs that seemed to lead deeper and deeper into a tangled web of criminal activity. Her short brown hair was pulled back in a tight ponytail, revealing the furrowed brow that signaled her relentless focus.

"Charlie, look at this," Sarah said, motioning for her partner to join her. "I think I've found a connection between Alex Thompson and the offshore accounts we've been tracking."

Charlie leaned over her shoulder, his salt-and-pepper hair casting a shadow on the screen. He squinted at the data, then nodded in agreement. "Nice work, Sarah. This could be our smoking gun."

As they analyzed the information, Sarah's phone buzzed on the table beside them. Glancing at the message, her eyes widened with alarm. "Damn it. We've got a problem," she muttered, showing the screen to Charlie. The anonymous tip read: "Your cover's blown. Get out now."

Adrenaline surged through Sarah's veins, prompting her to spring into action. "We need to move. Now."

"Agreed," Charlie responded, his voice steady despite the sudden urgency. They had faced danger before, but something about this situation felt different - more personal.

Sarah yanked the USB drive from the laptop, hurriedly stuffing it into her pocket along with other pieces of critical evidence. As she did so, her mind raced, trying to piece together who might have discovered their investigation. Was it a mole within the department? Or someone closer to the criminals they were pursuing?

"Grab anything sensitive," Charlie instructed, quickly wiping down surfaces and collecting any stray documents. He knew that leaving behind even the smallest trace of their presence could spell disaster for their case – and potentially their lives.

Sarah's hands shook as she closed the laptop and shoved it into her bag, a mix of fear and anger bubbling inside her. Whoever had blown their cover was not only jeopardizing the investigation but also putting them in the crosshairs of some very dangerous people. Her gambling addiction had taught her that sometimes luck just wasn't on your side, but this felt like more than bad luck. This was personal.

"Ready?" Charlie asked, his eyes scanning the room one last time for anything they might have missed.

"Let's go," Sarah replied, her determination fueling her every step as they slipped out of the motel room, leaving behind the life they had built undercover. Ahead lay the unknown, yet they were united by a singular goal: to bring down Alex Thompson and his criminal empire, no matter the cost.

•••

The engine roared to life as Sarah turned the key in the ignition, fingers gripping the steering wheel with white-knuckled intensity. The motel's neon sign flickered above them, casting eerie shadows across the car's dashboard.

"Head north," Charlie instructed, his voice steady despite their precarious situation. "We need to be off the grid for a while."

"Right." Sarah's foot pressed down on the accelerator, and they sped away from the motel, leaving behind a cloud of dust and the remnants of their former lives. Each mile that passed beneath their tires was a step further away from danger – or so she hoped.

"Remember the cabin?" Charlie asked, pulling a folded map from his pocket and tracing a finger along the winding roads.

"Of course," she replied, recalling the remote hideaway they'd discovered during a previous case. Its seclusion made it the perfect place to regroup and strategize, hidden from prying eyes.

"Good. We'll head there."

"Charlie," Sarah began, her voice strained as she navigated the dark, twisting roads, "what if we can't shake them? What if they're already onto us?"

"Then we'll face them," he said firmly, meeting her worried gaze with a reassuring nod. "Together."

As the miles disappeared behind them and the cityscape gave way to dense forest, Sarah couldn't help but feel the weight of her past decisions bearing down on her. Her gambling addiction had cost her dearly, both personally and professionally, and yet here she was, rolling the dice once more in pursuit of justice.

"Hey," Charlie said gently, pulling her from her thoughts. "You okay?"

"Fine," she lied, swallowing hard against the lump in her throat. "Just focused on getting us there safely."

"Good. Because I have a feeling we're going to need your sharp instincts more than ever."

Finally, the cabin came into view — a lone structure hidden within the shadows of towering pines. Its wooden walls seemed to offer a beacon of hope in their desperate situation.

"Here we are," Sarah said, cutting the engine and stepping out into the cool night air. The scent of damp earth and pine needles filled her nostrils as she grabbed their bags from the trunk.

"Home sweet home," Charlie remarked, surveying their surroundings with a watchful eye. "Let's get inside."

As they entered the musty cabin, Sarah felt a flicker of determination reignite within her. This would be their sanctuary, their fortress against the darkness threatening to engulf them. Together, they would face whatever challenges lay ahead and bring Alex Thompson to justice – or die trying.

•••

The morning sun filtered through the gaps in the wooden blinds, casting a dim glow across the cabin's dusty floorboards. Sarah sat at the small dining table, her fingers drumming against its surface as she scrutinized the scattered papers and photos before her. She could feel the weight of uncertainty bearing down on her – like a vise tightening around her chest.

"Charlie," she began, her voice strained and weary. "We need to figure out how we got made."

"Agreed." He pulled up a chair beside her, his eyes scanning the evidence they'd collected thus far. "There has to be something we missed."

A tense silence hung in the air as they pored over the documents, their minds racing with possibilities. The distant sound of a woodpecker echoed in the background, punctuating their thoughts like a relentless reminder of their vulnerability.

"Could it have been someone from the inside?" Sarah mused, picking up a photo of one of their suspects and examining it closely. "Someone who's working for Alex Thompson?"

"Possible," Charlie replied, rubbing his stubbled chin thoughtfully. "But it doesn't explain how they knew our exact location."

"Unless..." Sarah's eyes widened as a chilling realization dawned on her. "What if it was Alex themselves? What if they've been following us this entire time?"

"Jesus," Charlie muttered, running a hand through his salt-and-pepper hair. "If that's true, then we're dealing with someone far more dangerous than we initially thought."

"Which means we need to step up our game," Sarah declared, determination flashing in her eyes. "Alex Thompson wants to play hardball? Well, so can we."

"Damn right," Charlie agreed, his voice firm and resolute. "We'll find a way to expose them – and put an end to this nightmare once and for all."

As they sat amidst the scattered remnants of their investigation, Sarah couldn't help but feel a flicker of hope. The odds were stacked against them, but failure wasn't an option – not when justice was on the line.

"Alright," she said, her voice steady and unwavering. "Let's get to work."

•••

The wind howled outside the cabin, rattling the windows in their frames as Sarah and Charlie went about fortifying their makeshift safe house. The shadows of towering pine trees cast eerie silhouettes on the walls, making the already dimly lit space feel even more claustrophobic.

"Hand me those nails," Charlie grunted, his sturdy frame bent over a wooden board he was securing over a window. Sarah complied, her own hands busy tying tight knots in a length of rope, which would be used to secure the front door.

"Think this'll hold?" she asked, her voice betraying her concern as she glanced at the barricaded window.

"Should do," Charlie replied, driving a nail deep into the wooden board with practiced precision. "Unless Alex has a damn army at their disposal."

Their eyes met for a moment, the unspoken fear hanging heavy between them. They both knew that if Alex Thompson truly had been following them, they'd need more than just luck to stay alive.

"Check the perimeter one more time," Charlie instructed, wiping sweat from his brow. "I'll finish up in here."

As Sarah stepped outside, the cold air bit at her exposed skin, sending shivers down her spine. She scanned the darkened treeline, her pulse quickening at the slightest rustle of leaves or snap of a twig. Every shadow seemed to conceal a lurking menace, and she found herself gripping her sidearm tightly, knuckles turning white.

"Keep it together," she whispered to herself, forcing back the mounting paranoia. With each step along the perimeter, she reminded herself of her duty – to bring justice to the victims and put an end to Alex Thompson's reign of terror.

Back inside, Charlie had moved on to stocking provisions – canned food, bottled water, spare ammunition, and other essentials lined the shelves. As Sarah returned, shivering from the cold, he handed her a steaming mug of coffee.

"Thanks," she mumbled, wrapping her hands around the warm ceramic and taking a grateful sip. "No signs of anyone out there, but I can't shake the feeling that we're being watched."

"Can't afford to let our guard down," Charlie agreed, his gaze flicking to the locked and bolted front door. "Not for a second."

"Are we really prepared for this?" Sarah asked, her voice wavering slightly. "Taking on Alex Thompson and their entire operation?"

"Sarah, look at me," Charlie said firmly, his eyes meeting hers. "We've come too far to back down now. We knew this case would be dangerous – hell, every case we've taken on has been dangerous. But we've always made it through, one way or another."

"Because we had backup," Sarah countered, her thoughts drifting back to their support system – the colleagues they could no longer rely on, the friends who might already have been compromised. "Now it's just us."

"Then we'll make damn sure we're enough," Charlie declared, his voice filled with conviction. "Alex Thompson won't know what hit 'em."

As the wind continued to howl and shadows danced across the cabin walls, Sarah found herself clinging to Charlie's words like a lifeline. They were all they had now – each other, and the burning desire to see justice served.

•••

The fire crackled in the hearth, casting an eerie glow over the cabin as Sarah stared at the rough floorboards beneath her feet. She clenched her fists, feeling the weight of their isolation pressing down on her.

"Alright," she said, her voice low and steady. "We can't stay here forever. We need to find more evidence against Thompson."

Charlie leaned back in his chair, the aged wood creaking under his sturdy frame. "Agreed. But we'll have to be extra careful. No more shortcuts."

"Right." She met his gaze, determination flickering in her dark eyes. "So, what's our next move?"

"First things first, we need to track down any loose ends. People who've worked with Thompson, places they frequent, anything that could lead us to solid proof."

"Sounds like a plan." She chewed her lip, considering. "How do we do it without being spotted, though? They know our faces now."

"Disguises." Charlie grinned, rubbing his salt-and-pepper stubble. "Nothing fancy, just enough to throw them off our trail."

Sarah nodded, a small smile tugging at the corners of her mouth. "I always wanted to go undercover."

"Then let's make it count." He stood up, his sturdy boots thudding against the floor. "We'll start by scouting the town tomorrow night. Blend in, gather intel. Take it from there."

"Understood." She looked around the cabin, her thoughts racing ahead. How many chances did they have left before the odds caught up with them?

"Hey," Charlie said gently, resting a hand on her shoulder. "Don't worry, kid. We're gonna nail this bastard."

"Damn right we are," she replied, her grip tightening on the worn edges of the table.

●●●

The sun had dipped below the horizon, casting shadows across the cabin floor. Charlie paced in front of the window, his breath fogging up the glass as he spoke into the battered walkie-talkie. "Remember, no names. Just stick to the codes we discussed."

"Got it, boss," came the crackling response from their trusted ally on the other side. Sarah felt a flicker of relief - they weren't completely alone in this.

"Give us updates on Thompson's movements, any new leads." Charlie glanced at Sarah while he continued. "Stay safe, and don't hesitate to cut contact if you feel compromised."

"Will do." The static buzzed, filling the silence that followed.

"Alright, let's go dark now," Charlie said, flipping off the walkie-talkie before stowing it away. He turned to Sarah with a grim expression. "We're on our own for the most part now. Can't risk our superiors getting caught in the crossfire."

"Understood." Sarah gripped her own walkie-talkie, her knuckles whitening. Her heart raced, but she couldn't let fear derail her focus. Justice was within reach, and she'd be damned if she didn't see this through.

"Phones off," Charlie instructed, powering down his own device. The screen went black instantly, severing ties with the outside world. "No more social media, no more calls to family or friends. Not until this is over."

"Right." She hesitated for a moment, her thumb hovering over the power button. A pang of guilt washed over her as she thought about her loved ones. But she knew it was for the best. With a deep breath, she pressed the button and disconnected herself from her previous life.

"Okay," Charlie said, taking a seat at the table, which was cluttered with maps, case files, and empty coffee cups. "We'll need to be resourceful, pay with cash only, avoid security cameras, and keep a low profile."

"Got it." Sarah forced herself to focus on what lay ahead, not the growing darkness that enveloped them. They had to be smart about this, meticulous even. If they slipped up, it wasn't just their lives on the line.

"Tomorrow night we go undercover," Charlie said, his eyes locked on hers. "We'll hit the town, scout for intel, and take it one step at a time."

"Sounds good." She nodded, determination burning within her. It was time to turn the tables, to hunt down the truth that had eluded them for so long.

"Rest up, Sarah. We've got a long road ahead of us." Charlie stood, stretching his weary muscles before heading to his makeshift bed.

"Will do," she murmured, watching him disappear into the shadows. As the cabin's walls closed in around her, Sarah felt the weight of their isolation, the enormity of their task. But there was no turning back now. They'd come too far, risked too much. And she wouldn't rest until justice was served.

•••

The wind howled outside the cabin, a mournful wail punctuating the silence of the night. Charlie stood by the window, peering through the darkness. Sarah sat on the floor, methodically loading her gun. The cold metal felt strangely comforting in her hands.

"Y'know," Charlie began, eyes still fixed on the abyss beyond the glass, "I've been at this job for over 20 years, and it's never been like this."

"Like what?" Sarah asked, glancing up at him as she snapped the magazine into place.

"Being off the grid, out of touch with our team, our friends," he sighed, a hint of vulnerability creeping into his words. "It's... unsettling."

"Unsettling or not," Sarah replied, determination burning in her gaze, "we have to do this. We can't trust anyone else."

"True." He turned and leaned against the window frame. "But we can rely on each other, right?"

"Of course," she assured him, locking eyes with her partner. "We're a team, Charlie. We always have been."

"Then let's make sure we stay that way." He pushed off from the window and crossed the room, extending a hand to help her up. "You ready for this?"

"Ready as I'll ever be," she admitted, accepting his assistance and rising to her feet.

"Let's gear up, then." Charlie tossed her a black backpack stuffed with essentials - extra ammo, a change of clothes, some food and water. "Time to go."

Sarah took a deep breath, centering herself. Her heart raced, adrenaline pumping through her veins. It was time to face the unknown.

"Okay," she whispered, zipping up her coat and pulling the hood over her head. "Let's do this."

They slipped out the door, leaving the safety of the cabin behind. The darkness swallowed them whole as they navigated the rough terrain, their knowledge of the town's layout guiding them like a compass.

"Stick close, Sarah," Charlie warned, his voice barely audible above the wind. "We can't afford to get separated."

"Got it." She kept her eyes glued to his back, following his every step. It was easy to lose oneself in the shadows, but she refused to let fear take hold.

"Once we're in town," he continued, his breath fogging the frigid air, "we'll need to lay low. Blend in. Keep our ears open for any leads."

"Understood," she murmured, her mind racing with thoughts of what lay ahead. They were on their own now, each step taking them deeper into the heart of darkness. But there was no turning back - justice demanded it.

•••

A single streetlight flickered, casting eerie shadows on the desolate alley. Sarah and Charlie stood beneath it, their breaths forming clouds in the cold air.

"Remember," Charlie whispered, his voice low and tense, "stick to the plan. Stay sharp."

"Right." Sarah's fingers tightened around her weapon, the metal cold against her skin. Her heart pounded in her chest, each beat a reminder of the danger that lurked around every corner.

"Let's move," Charlie said, stepping into the darkness. They made their way through the winding alleys, their footsteps muffled by the damp ground. A stray cat darted past, its yellow eyes glowing like tiny lanterns in the night.

"Place should be just up ahead," Charlie muttered, peering around a corner. "That's where our source said Thompson would be."

"Thompson," Sarah thought, the name igniting a flame of determination within her. This was their one chance to bring down the mastermind behind the criminal operation that had plagued their town.

"Stay close," Charlie warned as they approached the rundown building, its windows dark and lifeless. They slipped inside, the door creaking ominously behind them.

"God, this place is a dump," Sarah said, her voice barely audible. Dust and debris littered the floor, while cobwebs hung from the ceiling like tattered shrouds.

"Keep your eyes peeled," Charlie replied, scanning the room with practiced precision. "Thompson could be anywhere."

"Got it." Sarah's brow furrowed in concentration, her senses on high alert. She could practically taste the danger in the air, feel its oppressive weight bearing down on her.

"Wait... there!" Charlie suddenly hissed, pointing toward a dimly lit doorway. A shadowy figure emerged, their movements slow and deliberate.

"Is that..." Sarah's breath caught in her throat as she recognized the telltale features of Alex Thompson. She gripped her gun with white-knuckled determination, ready to confront the darkness that had haunted their lives for so long.

"Stay calm," Charlie warned, his eyes never leaving Thompson. "We need him alive."

"Right," Sarah whispered, trying to steady her racing heart. It was time to bring this nightmare to an end. They crept forward, their boots silent on the grimy floor, each step bringing them closer to justice.

"Thompson!" Charlie barked, leveling his weapon at the figure. "You're under arrest!"

"Ah, detectives." Thompson's voice was smooth and cold, like ice on a winter's night. "I've been expecting you."

"Expecting us?" Sarah thought, her mind racing with the implications. This was it - their moment of truth. And they were determined to see it through to the end, no matter the cost.

10

The casino's neon lights glimmered in Sarah's eyes as she entered the smoky room. She looked around, desperate for a win to pull her out of this rut.

"Detective Mitchell?" A1 - 2

"Detective Mitchell?" A familiar voice called out, pulling Sarah from her thoughts. She turned to see the bartender, a middle-aged man with salt-and-pepper hair.

"Hey, Pete," she replied, avoiding eye contact as she approached the bar. "Just a soda, please."

"Sure thing," he said, handing her a glass of cola. "You know, I haven't seen you around here much lately."

"Been busy," Sarah lied, sipping her drink. Her eyes darted to the poker tables, hands itching for the feel of cards.

She knew it was wrong - the case demanded her attention. But her gambling addiction gnawed at her like a starving animal. She felt the pressure building, the need for a win consuming her.

"Hey, you okay?" Pete asked, concerned.

"Fine," she snapped, slamming her glass down and striding toward the poker table. The game had already started, and she slipped into an empty seat.

"Alright, let's make this quick," she muttered under her breath, her mind racing. This reckless decision, however, would cost her more than just money.

Unbeknownst to Sarah, her phone buzzed in her jacket pocket, its screen displaying a message from her partner Charlie: "Urgent lead. Call me ASAP."

As the night wore on, Sarah's losses piled up like debris after a storm. With each loss, her desperation grew, fueling a vicious cycle. Meanwhile, the unanswered text message sat heavy in her pocket, the lead slipping through her fingers like sand. "Come on, come on," she murmured, her heart pounding as she went all in on a bluff. Sweat glistened on her forehead. "Fold," one player announced, tossing his cards onto the table. Another followed suit, leaving Sarah and one other player locked in a tense standoff.

"Call," the last player said, revealing his hand - a full house. Sarah's heart sank as she tossed her cards down in defeat, her bluff exposed.

"Better luck next time," the man sneered, raking in the pot.

"Damn it," she muttered, slamming her fist on the table. The sound echoed through the casino, drawing curious glances from other patrons.

As she got up to leave, the weight of her actions hit her like a tidal wave - the money lost, the case jeopardized, and the trust of her partner fractured. Her addiction had clouded her judgment, leading her down a path of impulsive decisions that threatened not only her career but also the pursuit of justice.

"Sarah," Pete called after her, "are you sure you're alright?"

"Fine," she lied again, storming out of the casino, feeling anything but fine.

•••

The neon lights of the casino entrance cast eerie reflections on the damp pavement as Sarah stepped out into the chilly night. She shook off the last remnants of failure, clenching her teeth.

"Sarah!" Charlie's voice cut through her thoughts, and she turned to see him jogging towards her, his breath visible in the cold air. "I got a tip about a potential witness - someone who might know something about this case."

"Really?" Sarah feigned enthusiasm, her mind still reeling from the disastrous game. "Who is it?"

"An informant of mine," Charlie said, pulling out his phone. He scrolled through his contacts before handing it over to Sarah. "Here. But be careful, okay? I don't want you going off on your own again - not after what happened last time."

"Sure, Charlie." Sarah managed a small smile, but her thoughts were already elsewhere. The prospect of a new lead was intoxicating - a chance to redeem herself, to prove that she could still do her job despite her addiction. It was like dangling a winning hand in front of her, daring her to take the bait.

"Alright," Charlie nodded, looking concerned. "Just remember, we're a team. We need to work together on this."

"Of course," she agreed, although her resolve was beginning to waver. She studied the contact information on Charlie's phone, her heart racing with anticipation.

Later that night, Sarah lay in bed, staring at the ceiling. The shadows shifted around her, forming sinister patterns that seemed to mock her weakness. Her fingers twitched, itching to pick up the phone and call the informant.

"Charlie doesn't need to know," she rationalized, trying to justify her decision to pursue the lead alone. "I can handle this. I have to."

She reached for her phone, her pulse quickening. As she dialed the number, she felt a familiar thrill - the same adrenaline rush that fueled her gambling addiction. But this time, it was different. This time, it wasn't just her own fate at stake. It was justice itself.

"Hello?" The voice on the other end of the line was cautious, wary.

"Hi," Sarah said, trying to keep her voice steady. "I'm Detective Sarah Mitchell. I hear you have some information for me."

•••

The streetlights cast eerie shadows on the damp pavement as Sarah approached the dimly lit alley where the informant had instructed her to meet. Her heart hammered in her chest, each beat reminding her of the risk she was taking. She swallowed hard, pushing down her fear and the gnawing doubt that whispered Charlie's warnings into her ears.

"Showtime," she muttered under her breath, stepping cautiously into the darkness.

"Detective Mitchell?" A figure stepped out from behind a dumpster, his face obscured by the hood of his sweatshirt.

"Who's asking?" Sarah replied, trying to sound confident despite the trembling in her hands.

"Relax, I'm here to help." The informant pulled back his hood, revealing a scruffy beard and wild eyes that seemed to dance with some hidden knowledge. He offered a crooked grin, which did little to put Sarah at ease.

"Alright then, what have you got for me?"

"Names, places, everything you need to nail this bastard." The informant handed Sarah a crumpled envelope, their fingers brushing briefly in the exchange. "But be careful, Detective. They'll be watching."

"Watching?" Sarah asked, her voice cracking slightly.

"Them. The ones behind it all." The informant glanced nervously over his shoulder as if he could sense their presence lurking in the shadows. "They don't like loose ends."

Before Sarah could ask further questions, the sound of footsteps echoed through the alley, drawing closer. Panic flared in the informant's eyes, and he disappeared into the night without another word.

"Hey!" Sarah called after him, but it was too late. He was gone, leaving her alone in the dark with nothing but a handful of secrets and an unsettling feeling of dread.

"Sarah, what the hell are you doing?" Charlie's voice boomed from behind her, making her jump.

"Charlie? How did you -" Sarah stammered, clutching the envelope tightly.

"Never mind that. I knew something was off when you left the station tonight." Charlie's face was a mix of anger and concern as he stepped closer, his eyes narrowing in on the envelope. "What have you gotten yourself into? You know we're supposed to work together."

"Charlie, listen," Sarah began, struggling to find the words to explain her actions. "I just wanted to get the information. I didn't think it would be this dangerous."

"Your addiction is clouding your judgment, Sarah. You can't keep doing this to yourself, or to us." Charlie's voice softened, but the disappointment in his eyes cut deep. "You need help."

"Help?" Sarah scoffed, her fear morphing into defensive anger. "I don't need help, Charlie. I needed this information. And now we have it, don't we?"

"Sarah, you're not seeing the bigger picture here," Charlie pleaded, his frustration evident. "This isn't about one lead, or even one case. It's about your well-being. Your future."

"Fine," she spat, shoving the envelope into Charlie's hands. "Take it, then. Let's hope it's worth it."
As Sarah stormed away from the alley, Charlie stared after her, the weight of their partnership and the fragile state of their trust hanging heavy on his shoulders.

•••

Rain splattered the windshield as Sarah sat in her car, gripping the steering wheel with white knuckles. The argument with Charlie played on a loop in her mind, his words echoing like a broken record.
"Sarah, your addiction is clouding your judgment."

"Charlie, I can handle it," she snapped, her voice shaking, betraying her emotions.

"Can you really?" he shot back, the anger simmering beneath the surface. "Or are you just telling yourself that so you don't have to face the truth?"

"Damn it, Charlie!" Sarah slammed her fist onto the dashboard, frustration boiling over. "I'm doing my job. I'm getting results. Why can't you see that?"

"Because I care about you!" His voice cracked, the concern breaking through. "You're gambling with more than just money – you're putting your life and our partnership at risk."

"Is that what you think?" Her hands trembled on the wheel, her thoughts tumbling over each other in a chaotic mess. "That I'm just some liability you have to deal with?"

"Sarah, no, that's not what I meant." Charlie swallowed hard, searching for the right words. "But we've got to be able to trust each other, completely. And right now, I don't know if I can."

"Then maybe you shouldn't," she spat, her heart pounding against her ribs.

The silence between them stretched out like an abyss, swallowing up any chance of reconciliation. The rain outside grew heavier, the drops hammering against the car like a thousand tiny fists.

"Fine," Charlie muttered under his breath, his eyes dark and stormy as he stepped out into the downpour.

"Charlie, wait!" The cry tore from her throat, but it was too late – he was gone, swallowed by the darkness and rain.

"Damn it," she whispered, tears stinging her eyes as she slammed the car door shut. The engine roared to life, drowning out the sound of her own breaking heart.

•••

The harsh fluorescent light in the dingy apartment flickered, casting eerie shadows on the peeling wallpaper. Sarah's knuckles turned white as she gripped the back of a rickety chair, her jaw clenched tight.

"Charlie, you don't understand," she ground out through gritted teeth. "I can handle it. It's not like I'm letting it get in the way of our work."

"Sarah, we've lost leads because of your actions." Charlie's voice was low and dangerous, his eyes boring into hers. "We're so close to cracking this case, but you're too distracted by your own problems."

"Maybe if you'd just trust me and let me do my job, we wouldn't be having this conversation!" She threw her hands up in frustration, her voice rising an octave.

"Trust you?" Charlie spat the words out, disbelief etched across his face. "You think this is about trust? This is about you putting our lives on the line for your addiction!"

"Addiction? You make it sound like I'm some kind of junkie! I'm in control, Charlie. I always have been." But even as the words left her lips, she knew they rang hollow, and the truth stung like a slap to the face.

"Control?" He snorted, shaking his head. "Your gambling has taken over your life, Sarah. You can't see what it's doing to you – and to us."

"Us?" Sarah felt her chest tighten, her heart pounding like a jackhammer in her ears. "Is that what this is really about, Charlie? Are you afraid I'll drag you down with me?"

"Damn it, Sarah!" His fists clenched at his sides, his eyes blazing with anger and hurt. "This isn't about me. I just want you to get help before it's too late."

"Too late?" She scoffed, her words dripping with venom. "It's never been too late for you, has it? Always the hero, swooping in to save the day."

"Sarah, this isn't –" Charlie began, but she cut him off with a bitter laugh.

"Face it, Charlie, you're just scared that I might actually be better at my job if I didn't have you holding me back!" She knew the words were cruel, but she couldn't seem to stop herself, the anger and fear spewing forth like a geyser.

Charlie stared at her, his face a mask of shock and pain, and for a moment, the room was silent except for the steady drip of water from the leaky faucet.

"Fine." The word was barely a whisper as he turned away, his shoulders slumped in defeat.

"Where are you going?" Sarah demanded, the anger in her voice replaced by a sudden desperation.

"Somewhere you won't drag me down," he replied, his voice cold and distant. And with that, he strode out of the apartment, slamming the door behind him.

"Charlie!" Sarah's cry fell on deaf ears as the heavy door echoed through the empty room. Her legs gave way, and she collapsed into the rickety chair, tears streaming down her face, her world crumbling around her.

•••

The rain came down in sheets, soaking Sarah through her coat as she trudged through the dark, desolate streets. Her mind raced with the echo of her own harsh words – words that burned like acid in her throat and left a bitter taste in her mouth.

"Charlie!" She yelled again into the night, but there was no answer. The only response she got was a distant rumble of thunder, mocking her futile attempts to call him back.

"Sarah, you idiot," she muttered to herself, wiping her tear-streaked face on her sleeve. "What have you done?"

She stumbled into a vacant bus stop, seeking some respite from the torrential downpour. The cold metal bench offered little comfort, but it provided a place for her to sit and reflect on the rift she'd just created between her and her partner – a rift that threatened to topple their entire partnership.

"Maybe I'm not cut out for this job," she whispered into the darkness, her voice lost in the howl of the wind. "Maybe Charlie's right. Maybe I'm just too damn reckless."

"Or maybe you're just scared," a small voice in the back of her mind countered, and for a moment, Sarah considered the possibility. Was it fear that drove her to lash out at Charlie? Fear that she would fail, not only as a detective but as a person?

"Either way, I've got to get a handle on this addiction," she thought, clenching her fists in frustration. "I can't keep jeopardizing everything I care about – my career, my relationships, even my own safety – just for the thrill of the gamble."

As the rain continued to pour, Sarah's resolve hardened. She knew she had a long road ahead, one filled with self-doubt and the battle against her own demons. But she also knew that if she wanted to salvage her partnership with Charlie, she had to face those demons head-on.

"Starting now," she murmured, pulling herself up from the bench. "I've got to prove to Charlie – and to myself – that I can overcome this addiction."

With a deep breath, Sarah stepped back into the rain, determination fueling her every step. The storm raged around her, but for the first time in a long while, she felt a sense of clarity amidst the chaos — a glimmer of hope that maybe, just maybe, she could mend the broken bond between her and Charlie and move forward together in their pursuit of justice.

•••

The neon sign of the community center flickered in the darkness, casting a dim glow on the rain-slicked pavement below. Sarah stood outside, her heart pounding like a jackhammer as she tightly gripped her umbrella. She hesitated, glancing down at the crumpled support group flyer in her hand.

"Face your addiction," she whispered to herself, steeling her nerves. "For Charlie... and for yourself."

With a shaky breath, Sarah pushed open the heavy door and stepped inside. The warmth of the room enveloped her like a comforting embrace, but the knot in her stomach refused to loosen. As she walked toward the circle of chairs, the buzz of hushed conversations filled her ears.

"Welcome," a woman with kind eyes and a soothing voice greeted Sarah. "We're just about to start. Please, have a seat."

"Th-thank you," Sarah stammered, choosing a chair near the back. Her hands were clammy, her thoughts racing — what if someone recognized her? What if they saw through her tough detective exterior to the broken mess that lurked within?

"Let's begin," the woman announced, silencing the murmurs.

"My name is Linda, and I'm a recovering gambling addict. This is a safe space where we can share our experiences and support one another on our journey to recovery."

"Hi, Linda," the group chimed in unison. Sarah watched as one by one, each person shared their story. A construction worker who had lost his house, a teacher who had stolen from the school fund, a single mother who had gambled away her child's college savings – each tale more harrowing than the last.

"Sarah, would you like to share?" Linda gently prodded, noticing her silence.

"Um, sure," Sarah said, her voice barely audible. "I'm, uh, I'm Sarah, and I'm a gambling addict."

"Hi, Sarah," the group replied.

"Until now, I thought I had it under control," she continued, her voice gaining strength. "But my addiction has put my career – and my partnership with my best friend – in jeopardy. I... I don't want to lose everything."

"Thank you for sharing, Sarah," Linda said warmly. "We're here to help you."

Over the next hour, Sarah listened intently as the group offered advice and encouragement. She found herself opening up more than she ever had before, pouring out her fears and frustrations like water from a broken dam.

"Recovery is possible, Sarah," Linda reassured her as the meeting wound down. "One day at a time, one step at a time. We'll be here for you."

"Thank you," Sarah whispered, tears of relief and hope brimming in her eyes. As she left the community center that night, the rain had finally stopped, replaced by a sky full of stars. For the first time in what felt like forever, Sarah felt a glimmer of hope – a belief that she could conquer her demons and rebuild the shattered pieces of her life.

•••

The following day, Sarah walked into the precinct, her heart pounding in her chest. The fluorescent lights flickered overhead as she approached Charlie's desk. He was hunched over, examining a stack of photographs from the crime scene.

"Charlie," she said hesitantly, her voice barely audible above the din of the busy station.

He didn't even look up. "Yeah?"

"Can we talk?" She fidgeted, scratching at her wrist, trying to find the right words.

"About what?" His eyes remained focused on the photos, his brow furrowed with concentration.

"Look, I... I know I messed up. I'm sorry." She paused for a moment, searching his face for any sign of understanding. "But I want to make things right."

"Actions speak louder than words, Sarah." He finally glanced up, his face unreadable.

"Okay. I'll show you." She took a deep breath, steeling herself.

"I went to a support group last night. For gambling addiction. And I'm going to keep going. I promise."

"Good for you." Though his tone was flat, his eyes softened slightly. "But that doesn't change what's happened."

Sarah clenched her fists, trying to contain the hurt that threatened to spill out. "I know it doesn't. But I'm trying, Charlie. I really am."

"Trying isn't always enough." He sighed, running a hand through his salt-and-pepper hair. "We've lost leads, and our suspect is still out there. You have to do better, Sarah."

"Please, just give me another chance," she pleaded, desperation lacing her voice. "I won't let you down again."

"Fine." There was an edge to his voice as he handed her one of the photographs. "But this is your last shot, Sarah. You mess up again, and I'm done."

"Thank you," she whispered, gripping the photograph tightly. "I won't let you down."

"See that you don't." He turned away from her, his jaw tense with frustration.

As Sarah stared at the photo of the crime scene, the grisly details leaping out at her, she knew that this was her last chance to prove herself not only to Charlie, but to herself. She had to confront her demons, for her career, her partnership, and ultimately, for justice.

With a renewed sense of determination, Sarah set to work, poring over the evidence alongside Charlie in tense silence. The weight of their fractured partnership hung heavy in the air, an unspoken reminder of just how much was at stake.

As the day wore on and the shadows lengthened, Sarah couldn't help but wonder if they would ever find their way back to one another – or if they were destined to remain divided by the ghosts of her past mistakes.

"Let's call it a day," Charlie said tersely, breaking the oppressive quiet that had settled between them.

"Alright," Sarah replied, gathering her things. As she walked out into the fading light of the evening, she couldn't shake the feeling that everything hung in the balance, both her partnership with Charlie and their pursuit of justice.

"Tomorrow," she whispered to herself, steeling her resolve. "I'll make this right. I have to."

11

The flickering lamp cast eerie shadows on the peeling wallpaper of Sarah's apartment. She sat hunched over her cluttered table, nursing a cold cup of coffee between her hands. Her short brown hair hung in disarray, and the bags under her eyes bore testimony to countless sleepless nights.

"Damn it all," she muttered, rubbing her temples. The case files lay strewn across the table, their contents an overwhelming reminder of the stakes at play. For a moment, she allowed herself to drown in the sea of self-doubt that had become her constant companion.

"Maybe it's just too much," she whispered into the empty room. The scent of stale cigarettes filled her nostrils as she ran her fingers along the edge of a crumpled betting slip, a bitter reminder of her gambling addiction.

"Sarah, you're losing it," she told herself, tracing the lines of her worn reflection in the window. The city lights twinkled in the distance, oblivious to her struggle.

"Am I really cut out for this?" she asked the darkness, her voice trembling. Her chest tightened with each failed case that resurfaced in her mind, threatening to suffocate her beneath the weight of their collective failure.

"Maybe it's time to give up," she admitted, feeling the heavy burden of the case pressing down upon her. Her breath caught in her throat as she entertained the possibility of walking away from it all - the late nights, the stress, the insurmountable odds. "Everyone else would be better off without me, anyway." The words stung as they left her lips, but in her heart, she couldn't help but believe they were true.

"Detective Mitchell, huh?" she scoffed, her once-proud title now reduced to something that felt like a cruel joke. The ghosts of her past mistakes crowded around her, whispering taunts and accusations.

"Sarah, you're a screw-up," she said, her voice choked with tears. "You've always been a screw-up."

The world outside continued to spin, uncaring and indifferent, as Sarah Mitchell sat alone in her dimly lit apartment, consumed by regret and self-doubt.

•••

As the silence of her apartment grew heavier, Sarah's eyes wandered across the room. They came to rest on an old, worn photograph that sat on a dusty shelf — her father in his prime, his detective's badge glinting proudly on his chest. He had been her rock throughout her life, believing in her abilities even when she doubted herself. The memory of his unwavering support ignited a flicker of determination within her.

"Damn it, Dad," Sarah muttered, clenching her fists. "Why'd you have to be so stubborn?"

Her father's voice echoed in her mind, gruff and reassuring. "Never give up, kiddo. You're stronger than you think."

"Am I?" she whispered, her voice wavering. "Or am I just too afraid to admit that I'm not cut out for this?"

The photograph seemed to stare back at her, challenging her to confront the truth. And in that moment, she knew what she had to do. She needed to face her addiction head-on, to acknowledge the role it played in her past failures.

"Okay, okay!" she said, rubbing her temples. "You win, Dad. I'll deal with this mess, but I need your help."

Sarah paced the room, her thoughts racing. She needed a plan of action, a strategy that would allow her to bring the criminals to justice while simultaneously confronting her demons.

"First things first," she told herself, taking a deep breath. "Let's tackle this addiction."

As she mulled over her options, a vivid image of her last visit to the casino flashed before her eyes. The bright lights, the cacophony of sounds, the mounting debt that threatened to crush her...

"Enough," she hissed, shaking her head to banish the memory. "I can't let this control me anymore."

With each step she took, her resolve grew stronger. She knew that this wouldn't be an easy journey, but she was finally willing to face it head-on. For her father, for herself, and for the sake of justice.

"Time to make things right," she said, glancing once more at her father's photograph. "I won't let you down, Dad."

With newfound determination burning in her eyes, Sarah Mitchell prepared to confront her addiction and redeem herself as a top-notch detective. The road ahead would be long and difficult, but she was ready to fight – not just for her career, but for her very soul.

•••

The last vestiges of daylight filtered through the blinds, casting a somber glow on the cluttered desk. Sarah clenched her jaw, the muscles in her neck tightening as she willed herself to take a deep breath.

"Okay," she whispered, steadying herself. "Let's do this."

Her fingers trembled as she picked up her phone, scrolling through her contacts until the name of a support group for those struggling with addiction appeared on the screen. The number stared back at her, a lifeline just waiting to be dialed.

"Come on, Sarah," she muttered, silencing the doubts that threatened to suffocate her. "You can't do this alone."

Her thumb hesitated over the call button for a moment before she finally pressed it. The line rang, and with each passing second, her heart pounded harder in her chest.

"Hello?" A gentle voice answered on the other end of the line.

"Hi," Sarah choked out, her throat feeling inexplicably tight. "I... I need help."

"Of course," the voice replied, warm and understanding. "What's going on?"

"I'm an addict," she admitted, the words tasting bitter on her tongue. "G-gambling. It's... it's ruining my life."

"Thank you for reaching out, Sarah," the voice said softly, offering a semblance of comfort. "We're here to help you."

Sarah closed her eyes, allowing herself a moment to bask in the knowledge that she had taken the first step towards recovery. As she listened to the stranger on the other end of the line, she knew that this was just the beginning – but it was a start.

"Tell me about your last time gambling," the voice prompted gently.

"Uh..." She hesitated, recounting the details of her latest slip-up. "I went to the casino after work, and... I lost everything. My paycheck, my rent money... Everything."

"Sarah, it's okay," the voice assured her. "You've made a choice to seek help today. That's a huge step forward."

"Thank you," she murmured, feeling a small weight lift from her shoulders. "I just... I need to get better. For myself, and for... for my job."

"Your journey to recovery starts now," the voice said with conviction. "We'll be here to support you every step of the way."

"Thank you," Sarah whispered again, her grip on the phone tightening as she braced herself for the road ahead.

As they continued to speak, Sarah felt a growing sense of determination. She couldn't change the past, but she could shape her future – and she would do everything in her power to ensure that it was one free of addiction.

•••

Sarah's fingers trembled as she held the phone to her ear, the dial tone ringing hollow in the quiet apartment. Her heart pounded, a wild drumbeat echoing through her chest.

"Come on," she whispered, her voice barely audible. "Please pick up."

The silence that followed each ring was agonizing, doubts and fears swirling in her mind like storm clouds. Was she strong enough to overcome her addiction? Had she already ruined her career beyond repair?

"Hello," a warm voice finally answered, cutting through the haze of Sarah's thoughts. "Addiction Support Group hotline. How can I help you?"

"Hi," Sarah replied, her voice wavering slightly. "I... I need help."

"Of course," the voice said kindly. "You've taken a brave step by calling. Tell me what's going on."

Sarah hesitated for a moment, swallowing the lump in her throat. "I'm a detective," she began, her words slow and measured. "I have a gambling problem, and it's... it's affecting my work. My life."

"Thank you for sharing that with me," the stranger responded gently. "It's never easy to admit when we're struggling, but it's an important part of the healing process."

Sarah nodded, though the person on the other end couldn't see. The simple act of speaking her truth aloud felt like a balm, soothing the raw edges of her soul.

"Have you ever tried to get help before?" the voice asked.

"No," she admitted, a note of shame creeping into her response. "I always thought I could handle it on my own."

"Many people think that way at first," the stranger reassured her. "But reaching out for support is a strength, not a weakness."

"Thank you," Sarah murmured, feeling a small weight lift from her shoulders.

"Let's talk about some resources that could help you," the voice suggested. "There are meetings, therapy options, and other forms of support available to you."

"Okay," Sarah agreed, the flicker of hope within her growing stronger. "I'm ready."

As they continued to speak, Sarah found solace in the understanding and support of a stranger. It was a lifeline she desperately needed – a reminder that she wasn't alone in her struggles.

"Your journey to recovery starts now," the voice said with conviction. "We'll be here to support you every step of the way."

"Thank you," Sarah whispered again, her grip on the phone tightening as she braced herself for the road ahead.

•••

The voice on the other end of the line softened, as if sensing Sarah's need for reassurance. "I know someone who was in a similar situation," they began. "A brilliant detective, much like yourself. He struggled with alcoholism, and it nearly destroyed his career."

Sarah's eyes widened, her heart pounding at the familiarity of the story. "What happened to him?"

"Eventually, he hit rock bottom and realized he needed help. With support from his friends and colleagues, he found his way back. Now, he's one of our most respected officers."

"Really?" Sarah asked, her voice barely audible as she leaned closer to the phone.

"Absolutely," the stranger affirmed. "And there are countless others who have overcome their addictions and turned their lives around. It's never too late, Sarah."

In that moment, something shifted within her – a spark ignited by the possibility of redemption. She clung to the stranger's words like a lifeline.

"Thank you," she whispered, her grip on the phone tightening. "That means everything to me."

"Remember," the voice continued, "the road to recovery may be long and filled with challenges, but there is hope. And you don't have to walk it alone."

Sarah felt her chest swell with determination. As the conversation drew to a close, she took a deep breath, ready to face the journey ahead.

"Good luck, Sarah. We're here for you," the stranger said before hanging up.

The silence that followed was deafening, but within it, Sarah found a glimmer of hope. She knew the battle wouldn't be easy, but she was willing to fight – for herself, for her father, and for justice.

"Alright, Dad," she murmured, staring at the photograph on the wall. "Let's do this together."

With every step towards recovery, she would prove that she could rise above her demons and reclaim her life. And in doing so, she would finally become the detective her father had always believed she could be.

•••

The flickering light of the computer screen cast eerie shadows across Sarah's face as she began her research. Her fingertips danced over the keyboard, each click and clack echoing through the dimly lit apartment.

"Local addiction treatment centers..." she muttered under her breath, her eyes scanning the search results with a laser-like focus.

"Hey Siri," she called out, pulling up a notepad app on her phone. "Make a new note titled 'Steps to Recovery.'"

"Creating a new note titled 'Steps to Recovery,'" Siri replied in that familiar robotic tone.

"Step one," Sarah dictated, her voice firm and determined. "Find a local therapy center specializing in gambling addiction."

"Step two," she continued, "join a support group for fellow addicts."

"Step three," she added after a brief pause, "develop healthy coping mechanisms to replace gambling."

"Got it," Siri responded, faithfully recording Sarah's words.

She dove deeper into her online search, scrutinizing every website she came across. Each potential therapy option was carefully considered, weighing the pros and cons in her mind. She knew that selecting the right treatment center would be crucial to her recovery.

"Sarah," she whispered to herself, "you can do this. You have to do this."

As she scrolled through page after page of information, her determination only grew stronger. The faces of those who had successfully overcome their addictions stared back at her from testimonials and success stories – a beacon of hope amidst a sea of despair.

"Look at them," she thought, her heart swelling with inspiration. "If they can do it, so can I."

Eventually, Sarah settled on a nearby treatment center with high success rates and glowing reviews. It offered individual therapy sessions, group counseling, and even workshops on developing healthier habits. This place seemed like the perfect fit for her needs.

"Alright," she said aloud, her voice resolute. "This is the one."

"Step four," she instructed Siri, "schedule an appointment with the chosen therapy center."

"Adding 'Schedule an appointment with the chosen therapy center' to 'Steps to Recovery,'" Siri confirmed.

"Thank you, Siri," Sarah replied, a small smile playing on her lips. For the first time in what felt like ages, she allowed herself to feel hopeful about her future.

"Let's do this, Dad," she whispered, glancing once more at the photograph of her late father. "Together, we'll overcome this addiction and get back on track. I promise."

•••

The mirror was cracked, a spiderweb of imperfections that marred Sarah's reflection. She stared back at herself, eyes resolute and full of fire. Her hands clenched into fists, nails digging into her palms as she took a deep breath.

"Alright, Sarah," she said aloud, voice shaking slightly but determination undeterred. "You can do this."

Her heart pounded in her chest, the rhythm syncing with the mantra looping through her mind: I will overcome this addiction. I will regain control of my life.

"Step five," she murmured to herself, "face every challenge head-on."

Sarah's fingers twitched, itching for the familiar sensation of a deck of cards or the weight of a poker chip. Instead, she gripped the edge of the bathroom sink, knuckles turning white.

"Focus on what matters," she whispered, forcing herself to concentrate on the task at hand – solving the case and redeeming herself.

"Charlie's counting on you," she reminded herself, thinking of her partner and mentor. He had always believed in her, even when she didn't believe in herself.

"Ready?" she asked her reflection, meeting her own gaze with unyielding conviction.

"Ready," she answered, nodding firmly.

One last deep breath, and Sarah stepped away from the mirror. The apartment door loomed ahead, a barrier between her old life and the fresh start she was determined to forge. As she reached for the doorknob, she felt the weight of her past mistakes begin to lift from her shoulders.

"Goodbye, addiction," she declared, opening the door and stepping into the hallway. "Hello, redemption."

Sunlight streamed through the window, casting long shadows across the worn carpet. It was a new day, and Sarah Mitchell was ready to face it head-on.

12

The rain pelted the windows of the dimly lit diner, casting distorted shadows on the cracked leather booth where Sarah and Charlie sat. They huddled around two steaming mugs of coffee, its bitter aroma filling the air. Sarah's eyes were puffy, her red-rimmed gaze fixed on the swirling liquid in her cup.

"Charlie, I need to say something." Her voice trembled slightly.

"Go ahead, Sarah," he replied, his aging face softened by concern.

"I'm sorry for my mistakes—the gambling, jeopardizing cases—I know I've let you down," she confessed, a lone tear escaping her eye.

"Sarah, we all have our demons," Charlie said, reaching across the table to place a comforting hand on her arm. "You're only human."

"Still, I wish I could take it all back."
"Regret won't change the past, but it can help us grow," he advised, his eyes a mix of wisdom and empathy.
"Thank you, Charlie," she whispered, brushing away her tears. The gratitude in her voice was palpable.
"Look at us," Charlie mused, "two battered detectives, seeking solace in a run-down diner."
"Wouldn't trade it for anything," Sarah quipped, cracking a small smile.
"Neither would I." He grinned back, taking a sip of his lukewarm coffee. It tasted like burnt rubber, but he'd had worse. "Our partnership has been one hell of a ride, hasn't it?"
"Definitely," Sarah agreed, recalling the countless late nights and dangerous situations they'd faced together. "I don't know if I'd be here without you."

"Ah, you'd manage just fine," Charlie dismissed modestly, but his heart swelled with pride. "We've always had each other's backs. That's what makes us such a great team."

"Remember the Harris case?" Sarah asked, the memory surfacing like a specter. "I was so sure I could get that confession on my own."

"Stubborn as a mule," Charlie chuckled. "But you learned to trust me after that, and we nailed him together."

"Trust is everything in this line of work," she said, gripping her mug tighter, as if seeking warmth from its ceramic embrace.

"Damn straight," he agreed, his gaze meeting hers with a renewed sense of determination. "We've got each other, Sarah. And that's what'll get us through whatever comes next."

"Here's to us," she raised her mug in a toast, her eyes reflecting both gratitude and resolve.

"Here's to us," Charlie echoed, clinking his mug against hers, the sound a beacon in the stormy night.

• • •

The rain pattered against the window, a melancholic symphony accompanying their conversation. Sarah's gaze drifted to the droplets racing down the glass, her thoughts as tangled as the rivulets on the pane.

"Charlie," she began hesitantly, her voice barely above a whisper. "There's something I need to tell you."

"Sure, what is it?" His brows furrowed with concern, sensing the gravity of her words.

"I've been struggling," she confessed, wringing her hands in her lap. "With addiction... Gambling."

"Sarah..." Charlie's heart tightened at her revelation. He had suspected, but hearing her admit it was like a punch to the gut. "Every time I think I have it under control, I fall back in," she continued, staring down at her trembling fingers. "I'm determined to overcome it, for this case and for myself."

"Hey, look at me." Charlie reached out, lifting her chin so their eyes met. "We're in this together, remember? You don't have to face this alone."

"Thank you, Charlie," Sarah whispered, her eyes shimmering with unshed tears. "But I'm scared it'll ruin our progress. What if my weakness jeopardizes everything?"

"Listen," he said firmly, his grip on her chin gentle yet unwavering. "You're strong, Sarah. And we'll overcome this together, just like every other challenge we've faced."

"Promise?" she asked, her voice barely audible over the rain.

"Promise." His eyes locked onto hers, conveying the certainty that she desperately needed. "You're not just my partner; you're family. I'll stand by you through thick and thin."

"Thanks, Charlie," she murmured, choking back a sob. "I needed to hear that."

"Anytime, kid," he replied softly, releasing her chin and giving her hand a reassuring squeeze. "Now let's focus on the task at hand, together."

"Right," she nodded, wiping away a stray tear that had escaped her defenses. "Together."

As they leaned into each other for support, the rain continued its steady descent, washing away their doubts and fears, leaving them with a renewed sense of determination.

•••

Raindrops splattered against the car window, blurring the streetlights outside into streaks of amber. The air inside the vehicle was heavy with tension and the weight of their conversation. Sarah studied her reflection in the window, her face a mixture of resolve and vulnerability.

"Okay," she said, leaning forward and pulling her notebook out from the glove compartment. "We need a plan to take down Alex Thompson and expose this whole operation."

"Agreed," Charlie nodded, his jaw set in determination. "But we've got limited resources and have to be discreet."

"Right," Sarah replied, flipping through her notes. "We can't count on anyone else for now. It's just you and me, like always."

"Two partners against one criminal mastermind," Charlie mused, trying to lighten the mood. "Should be a piece of cake."

"Let's not underestimate him," she warned, shooting him a glance. "He's cunning and ruthless. We'll need to think outside the box."

"Alright," he conceded, folding his arms across his chest. "So what's our first move?"

Sarah traced her finger along the page, trying to connect the dots. "Well, we need more evidence. Something solid that we can use against him."

"Maybe...," she hesitated, then looked up with a spark in her eyes, "we infiltrate the organization ourselves. Undercover."

"Undercover?" Charlie raised an eyebrow, surprised by her bold idea. "That's risky, but it might just work. If we can get inside, we could gather all the intel we need to dismantle the operation."

"Exactly," Sarah agreed, feeling her pulse quicken at the thought. "We play our roles well, and no one will suspect a thing."

"Still," Charlie sighed, rubbing the back of his neck, "it won't be easy. We've never done anything like this before. And we're already dealing with a lot."

"True," she admitted, her excitement faltering for a moment. "But I believe in us, Charlie. We've faced challenges before and come out stronger."

"Alright," he said, his voice firm with resolve. "Let's do it. Let's go undercover and bring Alex Thompson down."

"Here's to us, then" Sarah whispered, her heart pounding in her chest as she closed her notebook, ready to write a new chapter in their partnership.

•••

As Charlie's eyes scanned the room, he felt the weight of their decision settling in his chest. The dimly lit apartment was filled with the lingering scent of stale coffee and the hum of a distant siren outside. He glanced at Sarah, her face etched with determination, and knew there was no turning back.

"Listen, Sarah," he began, his voice tinged with concern as he leaned against the kitchen counter. "I know we agreed to do this, but I have to be honest – I'm worried about the risks involved."

Her gaze met his, and she nodded slowly, acknowledging his fears. "I understand, Charlie. Going undercover isn't something we can take lightly."

"Right." He exhaled a shaky breath, running his fingers through his salt-and-pepper hair. "There's so much that could go wrong. We've got our careers, our reputations... our lives on the line."

"Charlie, I know." Sarah's voice softened, her hand reaching out to touch his forearm gently. "But we've considered other options, and none of them give us the access we need. It has to be this way."

He looked down at their intertwined hands, feeling both reassured and terrified at the same time. "And what about our personal lives? Our families, our friends... This could change everything."

"Maybe it will." Her eyes held a hint of sadness. "But I truly believe that bringing down Alex Thompson is worth the sacrifice. We owe it to those who've suffered because of him."

"Right?" She searched his face for agreement, her grip on his arm tightening slightly. "We can do this together, Charlie."

"Yeah, we can." He sighed, his resolve solidifying. "But let's not forget the toll this might take on our mental health. Going undercover means immersing ourselves in a world of crime and deceit. It won't be easy to shake that off when it's over."

"True." Sarah's brow furrowed, her thoughts no doubt echoing his. "But we'll have each other. We'll rely on our trust and partnership to keep us grounded."

"Okay." He swallowed hard, knowing the path they had chosen was fraught with danger. "Let's do it. Let's go undercover, bring Alex Thompson down, and expose this criminal operation once and for all."

"Here's to us," Sarah whispered, her eyes filled with a mixture of excitement and trepidation.

"Here's to us," Charlie echoed, raising an imaginary glass in the air, sealing their commitment to the mission ahead.

•••

The dim light from the streetlamp outside cast a subtle glow on Sarah's face as she stared at the corkboard in front of her, deep in thought. Clippings, photographs, and scribbled notes competed for space, each telling their small part of the story they were trying to uncover.

"Charlie," Sarah said, her voice barely above a whisper, "we need more information before we can infiltrate Thompson's organization. Our case has to be airtight."

"Agreed," Charlie replied, leaning back in his chair, the old springs creaking under his weight. "So what do you propose?"
Sarah tapped a finger against her chin, her eyes scanning the board. "We have informants and allies who might have valuable intel. We get in touch with them, gather everything we can — anything that'll strengthen our case." Her eyes met Charlie's, determination simmering beneath the surface.
"Good idea," he nodded, rubbing his salt-and-pepper stubble. "And I know someone else who could help us. A trusted contact within the police force. He's got an ear to the ground and might have insights or resources we can use."
"Perfect." The corners of Sarah's mouth lifted into a small smile. "But remember, we need to tread carefully. If word gets out about our plan, it could jeopardize the whole operation." "Of course," Charlie agreed, his voice laced with seriousness.
"We'll be cautious, but we can't let fear hold us back. Not now."
"Right," Sarah murmured. She reached for her phone, her fingers hovering over the screen as she considered who to call first. The gravity of their decision weighed heavy on her shoulders, but there was no turning back now. They had chosen their path, and they would see it through, together.
"Let's get started," Charlie said, his words a quiet resolve that mirrored her own thoughts. And with that, they began the delicate dance of reaching out to their contacts, each step bringing them closer to the heart of darkness they sought to expose.

...

The sun dipped below the horizon, casting a golden glow across the room. Dust particles danced in the fading light as Sarah and Charlie sat hunched over their makeshift workstation. The ticking of the clock on the wall seemed to grow louder, underscoring the urgency of their task.

"Alright," Sarah began, her voice low and steady. "We need to divide and conquer.

I'll focus on reaching out to our informants and allies; you contact your guy in the police force."

"Got it," Charlie replied, his eyes scanning the scribbled notes spread before them. He clenched his jaw, working through the stress that threatened to seep into his mind.

Sarah leaned back in her chair, arms crossed, her brown gaze locked onto the cluttered desk. She swallowed hard, her thoughts racing. "We have to set a timeline for all this. If we don't gather enough evidence in time, Alex will slip through our fingers again."

"Right," Charlie agreed, furrowing his brows. "Let's give ourselves two weeks. That should be enough time to get what we need without raising too much suspicion."

"Two weeks," Sarah repeated, nodding. Her heart beat faster at the thought of the challenges they'd face. She envisioned herself slipping through dark alleys, exchanging furtive words with shadowy figures – anything to bring justice to those who'd suffered under Alex's reign.

"Hey," Charlie said softly, a comforting hand on her shoulder. "We'll do this. Together. We've faced tough odds before, and we've always come out on top."

"Thanks, Charlie," she replied with a tight smile, appreciating the familiar warmth of his support. "I just... I can't let my addiction get in the way of the case. I owe it to everyone involved to stay focused."

"Look," Charlie sighed, locking eyes with her. "I trust you, Sarah. You're strong, and I know you'll stay the course. You've got this."

"Alright," she said, steeling herself. "Let's get to work."
As night fell, the city's underbelly came alive with whispered secrets and clandestine meetings. Sarah and Charlie stepped into the shadows, each on their own path, yet united in purpose. They would bring Alex Thompson down, no matter what it took.

•••

The rain pattered against the window, streaking across the glass like tears. Sarah and Charlie huddled over a cluttered table in their makeshift headquarters, the dim light casting long shadows on their faces.

"Alright," Sarah said, her voice low as she traced a finger along the map. "We'll split up to cover more ground, but we must keep each other updated every step of the way. Agreed?"
Agreed," Charlie nodded, his eyes meeting hers with resolve. "Constant communication is key here. We can't afford any missteps."

"Trust and teamwork," she murmured, thinking back on all they had been through together. She knew that without Charlie's unwavering support, she wouldn't have made it this far. He was her rock, her anchor in the storm.

"Exactly," he replied, his hand briefly covering hers on the map. "We've got each other's backs."

"Alright then," Sarah said, taking a deep breath as she straightened up, her gaze fixed on the circled locations. "We'll start by visiting our respective informants. I'll focus on the east side, you take the west."

"Understood," Charlie acknowledged, scribbling down notes on a notepad. "Two weeks, remember? Every detail counts."

"Every detail," she echoed, her heart pounding with anticipation. The weight of her addiction hung heavy, but she refused to let it control her. This case, these lives, meant everything.

"Sarah?" Charlie questioned, his brow furrowed with concern.

"Charlie...we're going to do this," she declared, determination coursing through her veins. "We're going to bring Alex Thompson down and expose this whole damn operation."

His face softened into a proud smile. "I know we will."

The room seemed to hum with energy, charged by their shared conviction. As the rain continued to fall outside, Sarah and Charlie immersed themselves in the plan, each detail falling into place like pieces of a puzzle.

"Alright," Charlie said, his voice steady and strong. "Let's get to work."

"Let's do this," Sarah agreed, her eyes gleaming with fierce determination. Together, they stepped into the night, ready to unravel the web of deceit that ensnared their city – whatever the cost.

•••

Rain pelted the windows, a constant reminder of the storm brewing outside – and within. Sarah studied the map spread out on the table before them, her eyes tracing the lines and circles that marked their targets. She could feel Charlie's steady presence beside her, his warmth a solid anchor in the chaos.

"Check your weapons," he instructed, his voice low and gravelly.

"Locked and loaded," she replied, confirming the readiness of her handgun. The weight of it in her hands felt familiar, comforting.
"Remember," Charlie added, looking directly into her eyes. "Stay focused. Stay sharp. We don't know what we're walking into."
"Got it." Sarah nodded, her chest tightening with anticipation. "Your first stop is the east side, right?" His concern was evident, even as he tried to hide it beneath a layer of professionalism.
"East side," she confirmed, swallowing hard. "I'll meet up with my informant there. See what they've got on Thompson."
"Good." He clasped her shoulder firmly. "And I'll hit the west side. We'll stay in touch, every step of the way."
"Every step," she echoed, the words binding them together like a promise.
As they gathered their belongings, Sarah could feel the adrenaline pumping through her veins, electrifying every nerve. This was it – the beginning of the end. The moment they'd been working towards all this time.

"Hey," Charlie said suddenly, halting her thoughts. "We've got this, alright? We know the risks, and we're prepared. We're gonna blow this case wide open."

"Damn straight," she agreed, steeling herself for the challenges ahead. A small smile tugged at the corners of her mouth, gratitude for her partner's unwavering support shining through.

"Alright." He exhaled slowly, his breath misting in the cold air. "Let's move."

With a final nod of determination, Sarah followed Charlie out into the rain-soaked night, each step bringing them closer to the truth – and the dangers that lay in wait.

13

The smell of saltwater and the distant creaking of carnival rides hung in the air as Sarah, Charlie, and their allies approached the shadowy pier. Night had settled, wrapping them in darkness, the atmosphere thick with tension and anticipation. This was the moment they'd been waiting for - the showdown that would make or break their case.

"Stay sharp," Charlie whispered, his voice barely audible above the crashing waves that echoed around them. "No mistakes, alright?"

"Got it," Sarah replied, her heart pounding in her chest like a wild animal trying to escape its cage. She couldn't afford any more screw-ups, not when her reputation on the force was already hanging by a thread. The gambling debts that gnawed at her thoughts could wait; right now, she had to focus.

"Fan out," Charlie instructed their team, his seasoned eyes scanning the area for any signs of movement. As they dispersed, he turned back to Sarah. "Remember, we're a team. We got each other's backs."

Sarah nodded, swallowing hard as she tried to steady her breathing. She knew how much Charlie had put on the line for her, and she was determined to prove herself worthy of his trust.

"Hey," Charlie said softly, catching her eye. "We've got this."

"Right," Sarah breathed, mustering a small smile. "We've got this."

As if on cue, the sound of laughter and screams from the nearby amusement park reached their ears, juxtaposing with the sinister mission they were embarking on. It was a chilling reminder of the world that continued to spin outside of their investigation - a world that was oblivious to the criminals they were about to confront.

"Let's do this," Sarah whispered, her pulse quickening as they moved forward into the fray. Tonight, there would be no room for failure. Tonight, they would bring justice to those who had slipped through the cracks for far too long.

•••

The salty air stung Sarah's nostrils as she crouched behind the worn carousel, its faded horses frozen mid-gallop. Her heart pounded like a drum, each beat a reminder of the stakes at hand. She peered around the edge, scanning the pier for any sign of the criminals they'd been hunting.

"Charlie," she whispered into her earpiece, "any movement?"

"Nothing yet," Charlie replied, his voice steady but tense. "Stay sharp."

"Stay sharp" echoed in her mind as she studied the surrounding area: abandoned carnival games with peeling paint, rusted chains clanking against their posts, and the distant laughter of oblivious park-goers. It all felt so surreal, like something ripped from the pages of a twisted fairytale.

"Alright, listen up," Charlie commanded through the earpiece, addressing their allies. "We need to cut off any escape routes. Andy, position yourself by the western exit. Maria, take the east. Keep your eyes open and your wits about you."

"Copy that," came the muffled replies, an undercurrent of determination weaving through the static.

Sarah's fingers tightened around the grip of her gun, sweat dampening her palms. Despite her history of bad luck on previous cases, this time had to be different. The debts that weighed on her conscience couldn't distract her now; she needed to focus, to prove herself worthy of Charlie's faith in her.

"Sarah," Charlie's voice broke through her thoughts, "you good?"

"I'm good," she replied, forcing confidence into her words.

"Watch your six," he warned, concern lacing his tone.

"Always do," she responded, taking a deep breath to steady her nerves.

As they waited, the cacophony of waves crashing against the shore and distant screams from the amusement park threatened to drown out the silence between them. It was in that moment Sarah understood that their world — the world of justice and darkness — existed alongside another, one filled with laughter and light. Tonight, they were tasked with protecting that other world, and there was no room for failure.

"Let's do this," she murmured, her resolve solidifying like steel. Together, they would bring these criminals to justice, even if it meant confronting the demons within themselves.

•••

Gunshots pierced the air, shattering the tense silence. Sarah instinctively hit the ground, heart hammering in her chest. Beside her, Charlie dove for cover behind a weathered bench.

"Sarah!" he yelled over the deafening roar of gunfire. "Stay low!"

"Got it!" she shouted back, adrenaline flooding her veins.

Bullets tore through the carousel, splintering wood and sending shards of metal flying. The creaky music of the ride stuttered as if responding to the violence. Sarah pressed herself against the cold, damp ground, eyes scanning for any signs of their assailants. Between shots, she could hear the distant laughter of park-goers, blissfully unaware of the chaos unfolding nearby.

"Charlie, where are they?" she asked, her voice barely audible above the fray.

"Can't see 'em," he replied, gritting his teeth as another bullet ricocheted off the bench.

Then, amidst the haze of smoke and debris, Sarah spotted Alex Thompson. Their piercing blue eyes bore into hers, cold and malicious. A group of armed criminals trailed behind, weapons aimed with lethal intent.

"Found them!" Sarah screamed, knowing that the stakes had just risen exponentially. "It's Alex Thompson!"

"Damn," Charlie muttered, his eyes narrowing. "We've got to take them down."

"Leave Thompson to me," Sarah thought, squeezing the grip of her gun tighter. She couldn't shake the feeling that this showdown was personal, that Alex held the key to unraveling the case that had consumed her life.

"Take out the others," she ordered, her voice steady despite the chaos around them. "I'll handle Thompson."

"Be careful, Sarah," Charlie warned, concern etched on his face.

"Always am," she replied, though her pounding heart betrayed her fear.

As the bullets continued to rain down upon them, Sarah summoned every ounce of strength and determination she possessed. This was the moment that would define her career, her chance to prove that she was more than just a detective plagued by bad luck.

"Let's end this," she whispered, and with a deep breath, she charged into the fray.

•••

"Charlie, cover me," Sarah shouted, her voice barely audible over the deafening gunfire. She glanced at her partner, the weight of their unspoken agreement settling on them like a heavy cloak.

"Got your back," Charlie replied, nodding determinedly. Their eyes locked for a brief moment, a silent reaffirmation that they would see this through to the end, no matter the cost. Adrenaline coursed through Sarah's veins, her pulse quickening as she steadied her trembling hands. Inhaling deeply, she felt the damp sea air fill her lungs - a fleeting reminder of life beyond the chaos.

"Ready?" Charlie asked, his grip tightening on his weapon.

"Now!" she yelled, her voice strong and resolute.

Sarah leaped from her cover, gun raised, eyes locked on Alex Thompson. Time seemed to slow as the distance between them shrank, each step bringing her closer to the confrontation she both craved and dreaded.

"Come on, you son of a bitch," she muttered under her breath, fueled by a mix of anger and determination.

"Watch out!" Charlie barked, firing off rounds to keep the criminals at bay. His voice was a lifeline in the storm of bullets, anchoring Sarah as she charged forward.

"Thompson!" she called, her voice laced with venom. Their eyes met once more, the cold blue gaze sending shivers down her spine. "Let's finish this."

"Been waiting for this, detective," Alex sneered, a twisted grin spreading across their face. They dropped their gun, raising their fists in anticipation.

"Your mistake," Sarah snarled, mirroring the gesture. As she closed the distance, her mind raced, calculating every possible outcome. This was it – her chance to prove herself and bring justice to those who had suffered under Alex Thompson's reign of terror.

•••

"Charlie, now!" Sarah barked, her voice slicing through the cacophony of gunfire and debris.

"Got your back!" Charlie's shots rang out in quick succession, each bullet an inch closer to their mark. The air buzzed with tension, heavy as lead.

"Thompson!" she called, every muscle tensed for the inevitable collision.

"Detective Mitchell," Alex replied, a twisted grin splitting their face like a knife. They tossed their gun aside, hands raised in anticipation.

"Your mistake." Sarah mirrored the gesture, fists clenched tight. Her mind raced, each heartbeat a countdown to impact.

"Come on, then!"

Their bodies collided like titans, all fury and power. Fists tore through the air, weaving a deadly dance of pain and precision. Sarah landed a solid punch, knuckles crashing against bone - Thompson reeled but retaliated, a vicious hook aimed at her temple.

"Is that all you got?" Alex taunted, eyes gleaming like ice.

"Hardly," she spat, dodging another blow by a hair's breadth.

"Argh!" Sarah's fist connected with Alex's ribs, a satisfying crack echoing through the chaos. The detective's thoughts were a whirlwind, fueled by adrenaline and the burning desire for justice.

"Nice one, Mitchell," Alex coughed, wiping blood from their mouth. "But it won't be enough."

"Shut up!" Sarah snarled, her foot connecting with Alex's knee.

Pain lanced through her shin, but she refused to let it show. She couldn't afford weakness, not now.

"Sarah!" Charlie's voice cut through the fray, a reminder that they were not alone in this battle. But his words were distant, drowned out by the pounding in her ears and the fire in her veins.

"Give...up..." she panted, each word punctuated by a blow. Her knuckles stung, her breath ragged - but she couldn't stop, wouldn't stop.

"Never!" Alex snarled, their eyes locked in a fierce battle of wills.

"Then you'll fall!" Sarah roared, a final surge of strength surging through her limbs. With a primal scream, she drove her fist into Alex Thompson's face, the force of the impact sending them both crashing to the ground.

"Stay...down," she whispered, chest heaving with exhaustion. But even as she fought for air, her mind raced forward, grappling with the shocking truth that still lay buried beneath this violent struggle.

•••

Sarah's fist connected with Alex's jaw, the satisfying crunch reverberating through her knuckles. She could taste victory, but her heart raced as she knew this fight was far from over.

"Didn't expect that, huh?" Sarah taunted, her breath ragged.

"Guess not," Alex growled, massaging their injured face.

"Get ready for more!" Sarah lunged forward, her body aching but her resolve unwavering.

"Wait!" Charlie shouted, his voice laced with urgency. But it was too late – Sarah had already moved in for another strike.

"Behind you!" Charlie warned, his eyes locked on the criminal sneaking up behind Sarah. The detective hesitated, torn between finishing off Alex and listening to her partner.

"Charlie..." The name fell from her lips like a prayer, her trust in him absolute.

"Trust me, Sarah!" he yelled, raising his gun. With a steady hand, Charlie fired at the criminal approaching Sarah, hitting them squarely in the chest. They crumpled to the ground, lifeless.

"Thanks," Sarah breathed, relief washing over her.

"Anytime," Charlie replied, a wry smile playing on his lips. "Now let's finish this!"

"Right!" Sarah nodded, her focus returning to Alex Thompson, who was struggling to regain their footing.

"Reinforcements!" came a shout from one of their allies.

"Perfect timing!" Charlie remarked, firing off a few rounds to cover their approach.

"Let's do this!" Sarah and Charlie exchanged a nod of appreciation.

14

The neon lights of the pier flickered and danced across Sarah's face, casting shadows that morphed with each step she took. The cacophony of laughter, chatter, and sirens from blinking arcade games filled the air, but to her, it was nothing more than white noise. Her heart pounded in her chest like a bass drum – anticipation and fear mixed in equal measure.

"Focus," she whispered to herself, scanning the crowd for any sign of Alex Thompson.

She knew they would be here, somewhere amidst the chaos of children running wild and couples strolling hand-in-hand. Each passing moment felt like an eternity, and Sarah could feel the weight of her past failures bearing down on her shoulders.

"Detective Mitchell," came a voice over her radio. "Any luck?"

"Nothing yet, but I'll find them," she replied tersely, adjusting the scratchy collar of her jacket.

As she passed by a row of claw grab machines, something caught her eye. There, at the far end, stood a figure bathed in the machine's electric blue glow. Their gaze locked onto her, piercing blue eyes betraying no emotion. Sarah tensed, recognizing the face she had studied for months – Alex Thompson.

"Found 'em," she muttered into her radio, swallowing the lump that had formed in her throat.

"Be careful, Sarah," warned the voice on the other end.

"Always am."

She approached cautiously, feeling the pull of her gambling addiction as she passed the enticing rows of slot machines. But this was no time for indulgence; justice was within reach, and she couldn't afford to let it slip away again.

"Hey there," Sarah called out as she neared Alex, feigning a casual tone. "Fancy meeting you here."

"Detective Mitchell," Alex greeted with a cold smile. "I've been expecting you."

"Really? Then you should know I won't let you get away this time," Sarah replied, her hand inching toward the gun holstered at her side.

"Bold words," Alex said, eyeing her movements. "But we both know you're not that lucky."

Sarah gritted her teeth, memories of failed cases and lost opportunities flashing in her mind. It was true; luck had never been on her side. But she couldn't let that stop her now. Her resolve hardened, and she kept her eyes locked on Alex's icy blue orbs, refusing to back down.

"Maybe," she admitted, "but I've got a feeling my luck might just be changing tonight."

•••

The neon lights cast eerie shadows on Alex's narrow face, their lips twisted in a sinister grin. "You really have no idea, do you?" they taunted, taking a step closer to Sarah.

"Enlighten me, then," she shot back, her hand gripping the gun handle more tightly. She could hear the faint hum of machinery from the nearby rides and the distant laughter of amusement-goers, but all that mattered was the figure before her.

"Your precious partner," Alex hissed, amusement flickering in their eyes. "He wasn't as clean as you thought."

Sarah's heart skipped a beat, her grip on the gun loosening ever so slightly. "You're lying," she growled.

"Am I? Think about it, Sarah. How many cases have slipped through your fingers? How many killers have walked free, thanks to your incompetence?"

Her chest tightened, memories of past failures threatening to suffocate her. She shook her head, trying to push the doubt away. "No, you're just trying to mess with my head."

"Or maybe," Alex continued, their voice smooth and venomous, "I'm showing you the missing pieces. The reason why it's always your cases that fall apart. Your partner was playing both sides, Sarah. And he played you like a fiddle."

Sarah's mind raced, thoughts flying in every direction. Could it be true? Was her partner really involved in all this? But she couldn't let doubt consume her. Not now, not when she was so close to getting answers.

"Even if that were true," Sarah said, steeling herself, "it doesn't change what I'm here for. You're still connected to this case, and I won't rest until you're behind bars."

"Ah, yes. The righteous detective on her holy crusade." Alex's mocking laughter echoed through the night, sending shivers down Sarah's spine. "Fortunately for me, you've never been very good at finishing what you start."

"Maybe I haven't," Sarah conceded, her voice unwavering as she locked eyes with Alex. "But one thing I can promise you is that I won't stop until I bring the killer to justice. And if that means exposing my partner's betrayal or cutting through your lies, then so be it."

Her determination burned bright, fueled by every failure, every disappointment that had led her to this moment. Alex Thompson may have planted seeds of doubt, but they wouldn't keep her from discovering the truth.

• • •

The scent of popcorn and cotton candy hung in the air, mingling with the faint, nauseating odor of vomit from a nearby trash can. The garish lights of the amusement area cast eerie shadows on the ground, distorting Sarah's surroundings into a surreal landscape. Her heart pounded in her chest as she continued to lock eyes with Alex Thompson.

"Tell me, detective," Alex sneered, their voice dripping with contempt. "Do you really think you can outsmart me? You're just a pawn in this game."

"Maybe I am," Sarah replied, her jaw clenched. "But pawns can still take down kings."

"Ah, and there it is," Alex said, shaking their head mockingly. "That stubborn pride of yours. It's always been your downfall."

"Save your breath," Sarah warned, her fingers flexing at her side. "Your mind games won't work on me this time."

As their verbal sparring intensified, Sarah noticed something glinting in the corner of her eye. She resisted the urge to glance directly at it, not wanting to give her discovery away. It was a small, sharp object – a broken shard of glass from a shattered bottle, lying near the base of a nearby food stand. Its jagged edge glistened ominously under the harsh artificial light.

"Face it, Sarah," Alex taunted, their grin widening. "You're out of your depth here. Give up now and go back to your mundane, pathetic life."

"Never," Sarah hissed, her resolve hardening. "Not until I expose you and every other corrupted soul in this town."

"Brave words," Alex scoffed. "But we both know you don't have what it takes."

"Keep talking, Thompson," Sarah said, a dangerous glint in her eyes. "You'll regret underestimating me."

Sarah calculated her next move, acutely aware of the hidden weapon within reach. It was a risk, but she knew it might be the only chance she had to gain the upper hand. And with each passing second, her determination grew stronger. She wouldn't let Alex Thompson win this game – not now, not ever.

•••

"Big mistake," Alex sneered, their piercing blue eyes narrowing as Sarah's gaze lingered on the hidden weapon a moment too long.

"Only one way to find out." With a lightning-fast lunge, Sarah reached for the glass shard. Alex's hand shot out in response, fingers clawing through the air mere inches from her wrist.

"Got it!" Sarah's triumphant cry echoed through the pier as she grasped the makeshift weapon. She spun around, adrenaline surging through her veins, and faced her adversary.

"Give it up, Thompson."

"Never," Alex snarled, lunging forward in a wild attempt to disarm Sarah. Their bodies collided, a tangle of limbs fueled by desperation and fear.

"Get off me!" Sarah yelled, struggling to maintain her grip on the jagged glass. Sweat trickled down her brow, stinging her eyes as she fought against Alex's vice-like grasp.

"Make me," Alex hissed back. Their teeth clenched together, the sound grinding like nails on a chalkboard. Sarah could feel Alex's hot breath on her face, smelling of stale cigarettes and cheap booze.

Focus. Control. Win. Sarah's thoughts raced through her mind like a mantra, pushing her body closer to its limits. She twisted, trying to land a solid blow with the shard, but Alex was relentless, matching her move for move.

"Your luck's run out, Detective," Alex spat, their voice dripping with venom. "Just like every other time."

"Shut up!" Sarah screamed, feeling the weight of her past failures bearing down on her. *Not this time. I won't let it happen again.*

Metal groaned and paint chipped as their struggle carried them into the side of a nearby attraction, the force of their impact causing the Ferris wheel to shudder. The taste of iron filled Sarah's mouth as she bit her lip, but she refused to relent.

"Is that all you've got?" Alex taunted. "No wonder you can't solve anything."

"Wrong again," Sarah growled through gritted teeth, her resolve hardening. With a final surge of strength, she managed to create enough distance to swing the glass shard toward Alex.

• • •

Grit stung her eyes. The smell of popcorn and saltwater hung in the air, a cruel contrast to the violence unfolding on the pier. Sarah's body ached from their vicious struggle, her breaths coming in ragged gasps.

"Give it up, Detective," Alex sneered, their voice a poisonous whisper in her ear as they grappled for control.

"Never," Sarah spat back, her fingers slipping on the shard's slick handle. Her mind raced, searching for a way to turn the tide.

"Pathetic," Alex hissed.

"Look again." Sarah's words were cold, her gaze calculating.

With a sudden pivot, she yanked Alex off-balance, using their momentum to slam them into the claw grab machine. Glass shattered, raining down like hail. Coins spilled across the floor, glinting like gold in the chaos.

"Ugh!" Alex groaned, momentarily stunned.

Seizing the opportunity, Sarah drove her knee into Alex's gut, forcing the air from their lungs. They doubled over, wheezing and vulnerable.

"Too slow," she taunted, her heart pounding in her ears. This was her chance; she couldn't let it slip away.

"Damn you," Alex choked out, their blue eyes blazing with fury.

"Save it for the judge," Sarah shot back, her grip tightening around the glass shard. She swung it toward Alex's wrist, cutting deep and severing their hold on the weapon.

Alex screamed in pain, clutching their bloodied hand. The weapon clattered to the ground, its metallic gleam now dulled by crimson stains.

"Gotcha," Sarah whispered, her victory earned by quick thinking and sheer determination. She stared down at Alex, broken and defeated. But even as adrenaline coursed through her veins, she knew this win came with a cost. For now, though, that price remained uncollected.

"Game over," she said, her voice steady and resolute.

•••

"Nice try," Sarah sneered, pinning Alex to the shattered claw grab machine. "Now let's talk."

"Go to hell," Alex spat, their blue eyes defiant.

"Start talking, or I swear you'll wish you were there." She pressed the glass shard against Alex's throat, her hand steady despite the pounding in her chest. "What's your role in the murder and the criminal operation?"

"Fine," Alex hissed. "You want the truth? I was just a pawn in their game."

"Whose game?" Sarah demanded, her grip tightening. She had come too far to be deterred now.

"Wilson Blackwood. He orchestrated everything. The murder, the drugs, the corruption." A bitter laugh escaped Alex's lips. "He used me and discarded me like trash."

"Blackwood?" Sarah's mind raced, trying to connect the dots. "But he's been dead for years."

"His legacy lives on." Alex's voice was laced with venom. "He groomed his successors to take over. They control the town from the shadows."

Sarah absorbed the revelation, her heart heavy with dread. It all made sense now – the elusive clues, the unending web of deceit. But the knowledge came at a high price, as she acknowledged the personal sacrifices she'd made along the way: sleepless nights spent gambling instead of seeking solace in loved ones' arms, friendships left to wither like autumn leaves.

"Damn it," she muttered under her breath. As the weight of her losses settled upon her shoulders, she knew that even bringing the killer to justice couldn't erase the damage done.

"Happy now, detective?" Alex sneered, sensing her inner turmoil.

"Hardly." Sarah's voice trembled, betraying her pain. "But at least I know the truth."

"Congratulations," Alex mocked. "Hope it was worth it."

"Me too," she whispered, the bittersweet taste of victory lingering on her tongue. But as she held Alex Thompson at her mercy, one thing was certain: she would never be the same again.

•••

"Enough!" Sarah snapped, her voice laced with authority. She gripped Alex's arm with a fierce determination and twisted it behind their back. "You're under arrest."

Alex winced as the pressure increased on their arm, but the defiance in their eyes never wavered. "So this is what justice looks like? A broken detective with a gambling problem?"

"Shut up," Sarah growled, struggling to ignore the sting of truth in Alex's words. She slapped handcuffs onto their wrists, the metallic click echoing through the amusement area like a gunshot.

"Detective Mitchell! Over here!" a voice shouted urgently from the crowd that had begun to gather.

"Stay put," she warned Alex before turning towards the voice. It was Officer Daniels, his uniform rumpled and his face flushed from running. He held up a pair of car keys, jangling them in the air. "I've got the squad car out front."

"Good." Sarah nodded curtly, grabbing Alex by the arm and hauling them forward. As they pushed through the throng of curious onlookers, she could feel the weight of their collective gazes, heavy with judgment and expectation.

"Never thought I'd see the day," muttered an elderly man from the crowd, his eyes narrowed in suspicion.

"Sarah Mitchell, bringing down a killer?" scoffed another, shaking his head disbelievingly.

"Focus," she reminded herself, steeling her resolve as she steered Alex toward the waiting squad car.

"Watch your head," she said coldly, shoving Alex into the backseat.

"Always so considerate, detective," Alex taunted, smirking despite their predicament.

"Can it," she retorted, slamming the door shut. The sound reverberated in her ears, a satisfying punctuation mark to the end of this chapter in her life.

"Good job, Mitchell," Daniels said, clapping her on the shoulder as the sirens wailed and the car sped away.

"Thanks," she murmured, her gaze lingering on the shrinking figure of Alex Thompson in the backseat. I did it, she thought, exhaling deeply. But is it really over?

"Hey," Daniels nudged her gently. "You okay?"

Sarah forced a smile, her thoughts still racing like a roulette wheel. "Yeah, just...thinking."

"About what?" he asked, genuinely concerned.

"Everything," she replied cryptically, her eyes drifting to the pier's edge where waves crashed against the shore. "The choices we make, the paths we walk..."

"Deep stuff, detective." He chuckled, trying to lighten the mood. "But remember, one case at a time. You can't change the past, but you can shape the future."

"Maybe," she conceded, allowing herself a small glimmer of hope as the last vestiges of sunlight dipped below the horizon. Somehow, she would find a way to rebuild what had been broken, to salvage the pieces of her life that remained.

"Come on," Daniels urged, guiding her gently away from the pier. "Let's go home."

"Home," she echoed softly, the word tasting foreign on her lips. But it was a start, she realized, a chance to begin anew. And with every step she took, the shadows of her past receded further into the distance, replaced by the promise of a brighter tomorrow.

• • •

The chatter of seagulls filled the air as Sarah stepped away from the chaos of the crime scene, the salty breeze tugging at her short brown hair. She could feel the weight of the past few months settling on her shoulders like a leaden blanket, but she refused to crumble beneath it.

"Detective Mitchell," Daniels called out, his voice barely audible above the crashing waves.

"Y-yeah?" she stammered, pulling herself back into the present.

"Good work today," he said, sincerity shining in his eyes. "You really came through."

"Thanks." Her voice was fragile, like thin glass. "But I couldn't have done it without you."

"Sarah—" Daniels hesitated for a moment, searching for the right words. "What's next for you?"

She stared at the ground, feeling the cool sand beneath her shoes. "I don't know. I've been so focused on this case, I haven't had time to think about anything else."

"Take a break, maybe?" he suggested, concern etched on his face. "You've earned it."

"Maybe," she agreed, though her mind buzzed with uncertainty. The gnawing void left by the case threatened to consume her, and the allure of the gambling dens whispered seductively in her ear—a dangerous temptation she knew she must resist.

A silence settled between them, heavy with unspoken thoughts. Sarah gazed out at the churning ocean, its depths mirroring the turmoil within her. "I just... wish things were different," she confessed, feeling the sting of tears behind her eyes.

"Life's a crapshoot," Daniels replied softly. "But we make the best of it, right?"

"Right," she echoed hollowly, forcing a smile that didn't quite reach her eyes.

As they walked away from the pier together, the sun dipped lower in the sky, casting long shadows across the beach. Sarah knew that though the case was closed, the memories of it would cling to her like a stubborn stain. She had brought the killer to justice, but at what cost?

"Hey," Daniels said suddenly, breaking the silence. "Wanna grab some dinner? My treat."

"Sure." She hesitated, then added, "Thanks."

"Anytime, partner."

The word resonated within her—partner. A reminder that she wasn't alone in facing the demons that haunted her. And as they left the pier behind, Sarah allowed herself a glimmer of hope, daring to believe that maybe, just maybe, things could change for the better.

15

The fluorescent lights flickered overhead as Sarah stood in front of her superiors, her heart pounding against her ribcage. Her hands trembled ever so slightly as she held the thick case file, a product of countless sleepless nights and relentless determination.

"Sir, I've gathered all the evidence," she began, her voice steady despite the nerves that threatened to betray her. "Every piece of the puzzle is in this file."

"Let's hear it, Detective Mitchell," Chief Thompson said gruffly, his eyes scrutinizing her from beneath a furrowed brow.
"Right." Sarah took a deep breath before launching into her findings. "Our killer targeted victims with high-risk behavior – gamblers, just like myself." She hesitated for a moment, internally struggling with the admission, but pressed on. "We found traces of the same rare, toxic plant on each victim, which led us to the killer's hideout."
As she recounted the details of their investigation, Sarah could sense the room warming up to her. She described the chilling scene they'd discovered in the killer's lair – the trophies he'd taken from his victims, the meticulous records he'd kept of their suffering. By the time she finished, even the most hardened officers in the room were visibly shaken.
"Excellent work, Detective Mitchell," Chief Thompson said, finally breaking the silence. "This is the kind of dedication we need on the force."
"Thank you, sir," Sarah replied, trying to hide her relief at the praise.
"Make sure everything is in order, then we'll organize a press conference to announce the arrest and prosecution. The public needs to know we've got this monster behind bars."
"Of course, sir." Sarah nodded and left the room, clutching the case file to her chest.

As she prepared for the press conference, Sarah couldn't help but feel her thoughts drift to her personal life. The sacrifices she'd made, the relationships that had crumbled under the weight of her obsession with this case. Was it all worth it?

"Detective Mitchell," a voice snapped her back to reality. "We're ready for you."

"Right." She squared her shoulders and stepped out onto the stage, facing the sea of reporters and flashing cameras. This was her moment of triumph, but the gnawing doubts in the back of her mind refused to be silenced.

As Sarah took her place at the podium, she forced herself to focus on the task at hand. She needed to present the evidence, make sure the public knew that justice would be served. For now, that's all that mattered.

"Good afternoon," she began, her voice clear and confident. "Today, we are here to announce the arrest and prosecution of a dangerous serial killer who has plagued our city for far too long..."

And as the cameras clicked and the reporters scribbled their notes, Sarah couldn't help but think that, despite everything, she was exactly where she was meant to be.

• • •

The applause still echoed in Sarah's ears as she stepped off the stage, her heart pounding. Flashbulbs burned behind her eyelids, and she took a moment to catch her breath.

"Amazing job, Mitchell," Charlie said, clapping a firm hand on her shoulder. His eyes, usually so calm, shone with pride.

"Thanks, Charlie," she replied, feeling a warmth spread through her chest at his words.

"Sarah!" Captain Adams strode towards her, his tall frame cutting through the throng of people. "That was quite a performance out there!"

"Thank you, sir." She straightened up, bracing herself for what came next.

"Your dedication and hard work on this case have not gone unnoticed," he continued, his voice serious but warm. "I'm pleased to announce that you'll be promoted to Detective Sergeant."

Sarah's pulse quickened. A promotion? The thought sent a mixture of elation and fear coursing through her veins. Had she truly earned it, or was this simply another gamble?

"Congratulations, Detective Sergeant Mitchell." Captain Adams extended his hand, and she shook it firmly.

"Thank you, sir. I won't let you down."

"Of that, I have no doubt," he replied, nodding before he turned away to address the other officers.

"Detective Sergeant Mitchell," Charlie repeated, a grin spreading across his face. "Has a nice ring to it, doesn't it?"

"Sure does," she admitted, allowing herself a small smile. "But it's also a huge responsibility. Can I really handle it?"

"Sarah, if anyone can, it's you," Charlie reassured her. "You've always been focused, determined, and one hell of a detective. This is just the beginning."

She looked into his eyes, searching for any hint of doubt. But all she found was unwavering belief in her abilities.

"Alright, then." She took a deep breath, steeling herself for the challenges ahead. "Detective Sergeant Mitchell it is."

As her fellow officers offered their congratulations and praise, Sarah couldn't help but think of the long road that had led her here. She'd made sacrifices, faced doubts and setbacks, but in the end, she'd emerged stronger than ever before.

"Here's to new beginnings," she whispered to herself, feeling the weight of her new title settle on her shoulders. And as she looked around at the faces of her colleagues, she knew, for certain, that she was ready for whatever came next.

•••

The buzzing of Sarah's phone on the nightstand shattered the fragile silence, its glow piercing through the darkness. She rolled over, knuckles white as she gripped the sheets, squinting at the screen. A text from her sister.

"Hey, just checking in. Are you free for dinner tomorrow?"

She stared at the message, feeling the familiar guilt tightening around her chest. She hadn't seen her family in months, always putting off their invitations. It had become something of a habit since the case began. But now it was over, wasn't it? She deserved a break. Didn't she?

"Sorry, sis. Maybe next time," she typed out reluctantly before hitting send. Her thumb hovered over the screen, hesitating. She deleted the message and started again. "Actually, I think I can make it."

"Great! See you at 7," came the response.

Sarah sighed and set the phone back on the nightstand, staring up at the ceiling. As much as she wanted to reconnect with her family, the thought of facing them filled her with anxiety. Would they see the cracks beneath her carefully composed facade? Would they still view her as the same woman who left them behind for the sake of her career?

"Maybe therapy wouldn't be such a bad idea after all," she muttered to herself.

"Did you say something?" Charlie mumbled groggily from his side of the bed.

"Nothing, go back to sleep." She kissed him softly on the cheek, whispering an apology.

The next day found Sarah sitting across from Dr. Allen, a highly recommended therapist. The room was cozy, with soft lighting and walls covered in diplomas and certificates. A faint scent of lavender hung in the air, soothing her nerves.

"Detective Mitchell, what brings you here today?" Dr. Allen asked gently, her pen poised above a notepad.

"Sarah, please," she replied, rubbing her hands together. "I... well, I just closed a major case, and it's taken a toll on me. On my relationships, my mental health."

"Tell me about it," Dr. Allen encouraged, nodding for her to continue.

Sarah took a deep breath, and the words poured forth, unfiltered and raw. The sleepless nights spent poring over evidence files, the pressure to catch the killer before they struck again, and the fear that she'd never measure up to her colleagues' expectations. As she spoke, Sarah became aware of the weight she'd been carrying, one she'd refused to acknowledge until now.

"Have you considered taking some time off?" Dr. Allen suggested after a long pause. "It sounds like you've been pushing yourself incredibly hard."

"I don't think I can," Sarah admitted, shaking her head. "What if something happens when I'm gone? What if there's another case I should be working on?"

"Sarah, you're human. You need rest, and you need to take care of yourself," Dr. Allen said firmly. "Your dedication is admirable, but it's important to recognize when to step back."

"Maybe you're right," she conceded, feeling a mix of relief and apprehension.

"Let's work on finding healthier ways to cope with stress and prioritize self-care," Dr. Allen proposed, scribbling notes on her notepad. "And remember, you can always reach out to me in between our sessions."

"Thank you, Dr. Allen," Sarah said, her voice cracking slightly.

For the first time in months, she felt a glimmer of hope that she could rebuild the bridges she'd burned in pursuit of justice.

• • •

Sarah leaned against the railing of the pier, her gaze fixed on the inky black water below. The wind whipped through her short brown hair as she allowed herself a moment to breathe. Despite Dr. Allen's advice, she couldn't shake the guilt that gnawed at her insides, threatening to consume her. She had put everything on the line for this case: her relationships, her mental health, and even her safety.

"Couldn't sleep either, huh?" Charlie's voice broke through her thoughts, his salt-and-pepper hair ruffled by the breeze.

"Nightmares," Sarah admitted, her voice barely audible above the crashing waves. "Keeps happening."

"Always does after a big case like this," Charlie said, his sturdy frame leaning against the railing beside her. "You start thinking about all the things you could've done differently, the choices you made." His eyes locked onto hers with an intensity that caught her off guard. "But you did good, Sarah. You brought justice to those families."

"Did I, though?" Sarah's fingers clenched around the cold metal railing. "I know we got the killer, but... at what cost? I can't maintain a relationship. Hell, I can't even sleep without seeing their faces." Her voice cracked, exposing the raw vulnerability she fought so hard to hide.

"Listen, kid," Charlie said softly, placing a reassuring hand on her shoulder. "This job, it takes its toll on all of us. We make sacrifices, but we do it because we believe in something bigger than ourselves."

"Sometimes I wonder if it's worth it," Sarah confessed, her eyes brimming with unshed tears. "All these sacrifices, all this pain... is it really worth it?"

"Only you can answer that," Charlie replied, his expression somber. "But let me tell you something I've learned in my years on the force: sometimes, it's not about finding happiness in the job. It's finding a way to carry that weight without letting it crush you."

"Is that even possible?" Sarah asked, her voice barely a whisper.

"Maybe," Charlie said with a sad smile. "But it helps to have someone there to share the load. Just know I've got your back, Sarah. No matter what."

"Thanks, Charlie," she said, grateful for his unwavering support and understanding. They stood there in silence, side by side, as the darkness of the night slowly gave way to a new day.

•••

The sun spilled over the horizon, casting a warm golden glow on the secluded beach. Sarah dug her toes into the soft sand, relishing the feeling of tranquility that washed over her as she stared out at the endless expanse of water. The rhythmic sound of waves crashing against the shore offered a soothing respite from the chaos that had consumed her life.

"Never thought I'd see you taking a break," Charlie remarked, appearing beside her with two cups of coffee in hand. His eyes twinkled with amusement as he handed one to her.

"Neither did I," Sarah admitted, accepting the cup gratefully. "But it was time."

"Good for you, kid," Charlie said, taking a seat next to her on the sand. "You've more than earned it."

Sarah sipped her coffee, her thoughts drifting back to the case that had consumed her for months. She felt a twinge of guilt for leaving the job behind, even temporarily. But as she took a deep breath of salty sea air, she realized that this brief escape was necessary - for her sanity and her ability to continue doing the work she loved.

"Charlie," she began tentatively, turning to face him. "Do you ever wonder how we keep going? After all we've seen?"

"Every damn day," he replied, his gaze fixed on the horizon. "But that's part of the job, isn't it? We shoulder that burden so others don't have to."

"Is that enough?" Sarah questioned, her brow furrowing.

"Sometimes," Charlie answered honestly. He looked at her, his expression serious. "But that doesn't mean we shouldn't take care of ourselves, too. We can't help others if we're falling apart."

Sarah mulled over his words, recognizing the wisdom behind them. Her fingers traced patterns in the sand, as she contemplated her future in law enforcement. The job demanded so much of her, but now, she grasped the importance of setting boundaries and preserving her mental health.

"Thanks for being here, Charlie," Sarah said softly, her voice barely audible above the sound of the ocean.

"Always, kid," he replied, placing a comforting hand on her shoulder. "Now let's enjoy this break while we can, huh?" Sarah nodded, allowing herself to be fully present in the moment. As they sat there together, watching the sun slowly climb higher into the sky, she felt a renewed determination to strike a balance between her career and personal life. The tide had turned, and with it, brought the promise of change.

•••

Sarah's first day back at the station felt like a breath of fresh air. The scent of freshly brewed coffee wafted through the air, mingling with the familiar hum of activity. She dropped her bag on her desk and glanced around the room, taking in the organized chaos that had once consumed her.

"Welcome back, Mitchell," Detective Jenkins called from across the room, raising his coffee cup in salute.

"Thanks, Jenkins," she replied, returning the gesture.

As Sarah settled into her chair, she noticed a small stack of envelopes tucked under her keyboard. Curious, she picked up the first one and carefully opened it. Inside was a handwritten note, the cursive script elegant and heartfelt.

"Dear Detective Mitchell," it began. "Words cannot express our gratitude for your tireless efforts in bringing justice to our daughter's killer..."

Sarah's chest tightened as she read the words of appreciation, each letter offering her validation and a sense of closure she hadn't realized she needed. She moved on to the next envelope, finding another message filled with gratitude from a different family. Each one thanked her for her dedication, for not giving up when others might have.

"Hey, Sarah," Charlie said, appearing at her side. "Got some fan mail?"

"Something like that," she replied, a small smile tugging at the corner of her mouth.

"Good," he said, patting her on the back. "You deserve it."

Later that week, Sarah stood in the grand ballroom of the city's finest hotel, surrounded by her colleagues and other distinguished guests. The event was an annual ceremony to honor the police department's achievements, and this year, she was among those being recognized.

"Detective Sarah Mitchell," the announcer's voice boomed through the speakers as she stepped onto the stage, her heart pounding in her chest. Applause erupted from the crowd, and she spotted Charlie in the front row, beaming with pride.

"Your relentless pursuit of justice and unwavering commitment to the victims and their families have made a lasting impact on our community," the announcer continued, presenting Sarah with a gleaming plaque. "Congratulations."

"Thank you," she said, gripping the award tightly. She looked out at the sea of faces before her, feeling both humbled and invigorated by their support.

In that moment, standing on the stage with the weight of her accomplishments in her hands, Sarah felt the dark cloud that had hung over her begin to dissipate. The recognition from the families of the victims and her peers provided her with a renewed sense of purpose, a reminder of why she had chosen this path in the first place.

"Keep up the good work, kid," Charlie whispered as she returned to her seat, his eyes shining with admiration.

"I will," she promised, her voice low but resolute.

As the ceremony came to an end, Sarah knew that there would always be challenges ahead, more cases that would test her limits. But she also understood now that she didn't have to face them alone or neglect her own well-being in the process.

"Ready for what's next?" Charlie asked, offering his arm as they exited the ballroom.

"Absolutely," Sarah replied, a determined glint in her eye. And together, they walked into the future, ready to strike that delicate balance between duty and self-care.

● ● ●

The sun dipped below the horizon, casting an orange glow over the city as Sarah stood on the rooftop of her apartment building. She leaned against the railing, the cold metal biting into her palms as she stared out at the sprawling skyline.
"Mind if I join you?" Charlie's voice broke through her thoughts, his footsteps echoing softly across the concrete.
"Of course not," she said, her eyes never leaving the view.

He leaned beside her, their shoulders barely touching, and lit a cigarette. "You did good, kid," he murmured, exhaling a cloud of smoke that drifted off into the fading light.

"Thanks, Charlie." Her voice was quiet, almost lost in the wind that whipped around them. "I just... I don't know if I can keep doing this."

"Doing what?" He glanced at her, concern etching lines into his weathered face.

"Chasing killers. Sacrificing everything." She looked down at her hands, the skin raw from gripping the railing so tightly. "I love being a detective, but it's cost me so much."

"Sarah," he said earnestly, "you're one of the best detectives I've ever seen. But you're right; it's a damn hard life."

She turned to face him, her brown eyes searching his for answers. "Did you ever think about walking away?"

"Every day," he admitted with a rueful smile. "But something always kept me here. The thrill of solving a case, the satisfaction of bringing someone to justice."

"Is it worth it, though? All the sacrifices?"

"Only you can answer that." Charlie flicked his cigarette away, watching the glowing ember arc through the air before disappearing into the darkness.

For a moment, they stood in silence, the weight of Sarah's decision pressing down on both of them like the heavy clouds overhead.

"I want to make it work," she finally said, her voice steady. "I want to find a way to balance my personal life with my career."

"Then you will," Charlie replied, placing a reassuring hand on her shoulder. "You're strong, Sarah. You can do this."

"Thank you, Charlie," she whispered, and together they stood, watching the last light of day fade into night, knowing that the path ahead would be difficult but determined to face it side by side.

•••

The waves crashed against the pier, a rhythmic soundtrack to Sarah's pounding thoughts. Seagulls cawed overhead, their cries mingling with the distant shouts of fishermen hauling in their catch.

"Sometimes I come here to clear my head," Charlie said, breaking her reverie. He leaned against the railing, the evening breeze tugging at his unkempt hair.

"Does it work?" Sarah asked, her gaze still fixed on the churning waters below.

"Sometimes."

A gust of wind brought the salty scent of the ocean to Sarah's nostrils, and she shivered, drawing her coat tighter around her. She knew she had made her decision, but the weight of it still pressed down on her like an anchor.

"Charlie?" Her voice was barely audible above the roar of the sea.

"Yeah?"

"Thank you. For everything."

"Hey, no problem." His eyes met hers for a moment and then returned to the horizon. "You know I've always got your back." Sarah released a deep breath, her chest feeling lighter than it had in months. She flashed him a faint smile, gratitude shining in her eyes.

"Ready to go?" Charlie asked, pushing off from the railing.

"Yeah," she replied, nodding once. "I'm ready."

As they turned away from the pier, Sarah took one last look at the endless expanse of water, the swirling currents reflecting her own turbulent emotions. The waves seemed to whisper a farewell, reminding her that endings were also beginnings.

"Let's do this," Sarah murmured, determination hardening her features as she strode alongside Charlie.

"Absolutely," he agreed, matching her pace. "Together."

Her footsteps echoed on the wooden planks, each step marking a new chapter in her life. The darkness of the night seemed less foreboding now, as if the shadows held not fear, but possibility.

And as Sarah walked away from the pier, she knew she was moving not just toward a new balance in her life, but also toward a future filled with hope and resilience.

16

The pier creaked beneath Sarah's feet as she trudged away, her shoulders slumped and legs feeling like lead. The sea stretched out before her, seemingly endless, its dark waters reflecting the turmoil in her heart.

"Another case closed," she muttered to herself, each word laced with exhaustion.

"Was it worth it though?" a nagging voice whispered in her mind. She shook her head, trying to silence it.

As her gaze lingered on the horizon, the waves crashed against the shore, their relentless assault mimicking the thoughts that plagued her. The salty tang of the ocean filled her nostrils, but it did nothing to cleanse her conscience.

"Sarah, hey," a familiar voice called out behind her. She turned to see her partner, Detective Mike Thompson, jogging towards her. "You alright?"

"Fine, Mike," she replied, forcing a smile. "Just... tired."

"Tell me about it," he said, panting slightly. "This case has been brutal."

"Brutal" barely covered it. The gruesome crime scene images flickered in her mind, unbidden.

"Hard not to think about it," he continued, following her gaze out to sea. "But we got him, right?"

"Right," she echoed, but the word felt hollow. Her gambling debts had piled up during the investigation, adding to her already strained personal life. The stakes had been high, and she'd bet everything on solving this case.

"Sarah," Mike said softly, placing a hand on her shoulder. "We're a team. We got through this together."

"Thanks, Mike," she sighed, her eyes never leaving the churning water. "I just wish..."

"Hey," he interrupted gently. "You don't need to prove anything to anyone. You're an incredible detective."

"Am I, though?" The question slipped out before she could stop it. "What did I really gain from all this? What did I lose?"

"Sometimes, Sarah," he said, his voice heavy with empathy, "we can't have everything. We make sacrifices for the greater good."

"Is it worth it?" she asked, her voice barely audible above the sound of the waves.

"Only you can answer that," he replied, giving her shoulder a reassuring squeeze before stepping back. "But just remember, you're not alone in this."

As Sarah stood there, staring at the vast expanse of the sea, she couldn't help but wonder if the victory was worth the price she had paid. And though Mike's words offered some comfort, she knew deep down that nothing would ever be the same again.

•••

The salty breeze licked at her cheeks, carrying with it the scent of ocean and the weight of the choices she had made. Sarah blinked back tears, struggling to keep her composure as the wind tangled her short brown hair.

"Damn," she muttered under her breath, wiping at her eyes with the back of her hand.

"Sarah?" Mike's voice reached her from behind, a gentle inquiry laced with concern.

"Fine," she snapped, too quickly, too defensively, but her thoughts were already wandering, pulled away by the garish lights of the amusement park rides.

"Take your time," he said, stepping back, giving her space.

Her gaze followed the colorful dance of the ferris wheel, its vibrant hues flickering against the backdrop of approaching twilight. The laughter and shrieks of delight from nearby park-goers seemed distant, swallowed by the darkness that consumed her heart.

"Should've been me" she whispered, rubbing her fingers together, feeling the phantom sensation of poker chips slipping through her grasp.

"Nothing you could've done, Sarah" Mike said, his voice soft but firm. "You did everything you could."

"Did I?" Her eyes flicked briefly to him, then back to the hypnotic spin of the ferris wheel. "My gambling, my past... it all led up to this moment, didn't it?"

"Your past doesn't define you, Sarah" he insisted, placing a hand on her shoulder. "You are an amazing detective."

"Am I?" she asked, her voice barely audible above the cacophony of the park. "Are these victories worth the sacrifices? My family, my sanity..."

"Only you can answer that" he replied, squeezing her shoulder gently. "Just remember, you're not alone in this."

She stared at the amusement park rides, their bright colors taunting her with the promise of happiness just out of reach. As the wind continued to whip around her, carrying with it the echoes of her choices, Sarah knew that nothing would ever be the same again.

• • •

"Damn," Sarah muttered under her breath, her fingers trembling as she fumbled with the zipper of her jacket. She finally managed to pull it up, pressing the edges together against the biting wind that seemed determined to invade every inch of her.

"Sarah?" Charlie's voice, a lifeline in the growing darkness, found her amidst the chaos of her thoughts. "You okay?"

"Fine," she lied, pulling the jacket tighter around her body. The fabric rasped against her skin, but provided no comfort from the icy tendrils of doubt that coiled around her heart.

"Let's grab some coffee," Charlie suggested, nodding towards a nearby café, its windows glowing with warm light.

"Sure," she agreed, following him without really seeing where they were going. Her mind was elsewhere, reliving the gruesome details of the case that had consumed them both for months.

"Black, two sugars?" Charlie asked, bringing her back to the present.

"Y-yeah," she stammered, realizing she had been staring blindly at the crime scene photos spread across the table. Richard Evans' lifeless eyes stared back at her, accusing.

"Sarah," Charlie's tone was gentle, but insistent. "Talk to me."

"Charlie, I..." she hesitated, swallowing hard. "This case... it's tearing me apart. My family, my friends – I've pushed everyone away."

"Hey," he reached across the table, covering her hand with his own. "We're gonna get through this, alright? You're not alone."

"But what if it's not worth it?" Her voice cracked, and she fought to blink back tears. "What if all these sacrifices, all this pain... what if it's all for nothing?"

"Justice is never for nothing," Charlie replied firmly. His eyes held hers, unwavering. "And you, Sarah, are one hell of a detective. Don't ever forget that."

"Thanks," she whispered, her eyes darting back to the photos. The blood-spattered claw machine seemed to taunt her, daring her to look away.

"Come on," Charlie said gently, rising from his seat. "Let's get some air."

As they stepped outside, Sarah felt the cold seep into her bones, stealing what little warmth she had found in the café. The wind howled around them, a mournful lament that seemed to echo her own uncertainty and fear.

"Charlie?" she asked softly, her breath visible in the frosty air.

"Yeah?"

"Promise me something?"

"Anything."

"Promise me that no matter what happens... we'll see this through to the end. Together."

"Always," he vowed, wrapping an arm around her shoulders as they faced the storm together.

•••

Sarah's heart pounded, each beat a drum of doubt echoing through her chest. She stared at the claw grab machine, its innocent facade now marred by the memory of Richard Evans' lifeless body. The colorful lights flickered in sync with her racing thoughts.

"Sarah," Charlie said, concern lacing his voice. "You okay?"

"Fine," she muttered, but her gaze never faltered from the macabre scene in her mind. Fine, she repeated to herself, a mantra that felt more hollow with each passing second.

"Look," Charlie shifted his weight, trying to break through her walls. "We all have doubts. It's part of the job."

"Is it?" she shot back, the words a bitter challenge. "Is it really? Or is that just what we tell ourselves to justify everything we've sacrificed?"

"Sarah," he sighed, rubbing his forehead in frustration. "You're an amazing detective. You've done so much good..."

"Good?" she scoffed, her eyes narrowing as her grip tightened on her jacket. "What good is catching criminals if I destroy my own life in the process?"

"Hey." His hand found her arm, a warm anchor in a sea of uncertainty. "You haven't destroyed anything. We've made choices to bring justice for people like Richard Evans. That matters."

"Does it?" she whispered, the question a ghostly presence hovering between them. "Does it truly matter when I can barely recognize myself anymore?"

"Sarah..." Charlie's voice was soft, almost pleading. "You've got to believe in yourself. Believe that what we do has meaning."

"Maybe I used to," she admitted, finally tearing her gaze away from the claw grab machine. "But now... I don't know. I just don't know."

"Then let me be the one who believes for both of us," he offered, his eyes filled with determination. "I'll carry that weight for you, Sarah. Just don't give up."

"Charlie," she breathed, touched by his unwavering loyalty. "I... Thank you."

"Anytime," he smiled, giving her a gentle squeeze before releasing her arm. "Now come on, we've got work to do."

As they walked away from the claw grab machine, Sarah's thoughts churned like turbulent waves, and though uncertainty still gnawed at her, she found solace in the knowledge that she didn't have to face it alone.

•••

The neon lights of the claw grab machine cast dancing shadows on Sarah's face as she stared at it, her mind racing back to the start of her journey as a detective. Flashes of victories and failures intertwined, merging into an unyielding, cacophonous memory.

"Remember our first case together?" Charlie asked, his voice low and steady, breaking through her thoughts like a life raft.

"Of course," she replied, her eyes flicking to him before returning to the claw machine. "We got that bastard who killed that young couple."

"Exactly. You were relentless. You always are." There was pride in his voice, but also a hint of concern.

Sarah let out a short, mirthless laugh. "Yeah. Relentless... That's one way to put it." The word echoed in her head, a constant reminder of the path she had chosen.

"Hey, you've done a lot of good, Sarah. Don't forget that." Charlie's hand landed on her shoulder, offering support.

"Good?" She scoffed, feeling the weight of every strained relationship, every lost friend, crushing her shoulders like Atlas holding the world. "The price of that 'good' is too damn high, Charlie."

"Sometimes sacrifices must be made," he said gently, though Sarah could hear the strain in his voice, too.

"Did I have to sacrifice my sanity, though?" She pressed, her voice cracking with emotion. "My marriage? My happiness?"

"Maybe not," Charlie admitted, his eyes searching hers for understanding. "But without those sacrifices, who knows how many more people would have suffered?"

"Damn it, Charlie!" she snapped, her anger finally boiling over. "I can't keep going like this! Every day, I fight my demons, but they're not just in the field anymore." She paused, her voice wavering. "They're in my head."

"Sarah," he said firmly, gripping her shoulder tighter. "You're not alone. I'm here."

"Thank you," she whispered, her eyes brimming with tears. "But I don't know how much longer I can keep doing this."

"Then let's take it one day at a time," he suggested, his gaze unwavering. "Together."

Sarah nodded, the certainty of Charlie's words offering a fragile hope amidst the chaos within her. And as they turned away from the claw grab machine, the reminder of their victories and failures, she clung to that hope like a lifeline.

•••

The sea stretched out before her, a dark and endless canvas. Sarah's heart ached as she stood at the edge of the pier, the wind tugging at her jacket. Her eyes flicked to the scars on her knuckles, each a jagged reminder of the battles she'd fought.

"Top-notch detective, huh?" she muttered under her breath, pride and regret warring within her chest. "At what cost?"

"Sarah," Charlie called out, his footsteps echoing on the wooden planks behind her. "You've done good work."

"Good work?" She scoffed, her voice barely audible above the crashing waves. "I've lost so much, Charlie... Can you honestly say it was worth it?"

"Look around you," he urged, gesturing toward the pier - the families enjoying their evening, the laughter of children riding the carousel. "This is what you fought for. A safer world for them."

"Safe?" Sarah shook her head, staring out at the ocean's inky depths. "Nothing feels safe anymore. Not even my own thoughts."

"Hey," Charlie said softly, placing a reassuring hand on her shoulder. "Remember that time when we busted that drug ring? You didn't back down, even when your life was on the line."

"Of course I remember," she replied, her eyes brimming with unshed tears. "But all these victories... They have a price, don't they?"

"Every choice has consequences," he acknowledged. "But without you, who knows how many more people would've been hurt?"

"Maybe... But sometimes I wonder if it's enough," she admitted, her gaze locked on the horizon, where the sun bled into the sea. "If this path I've chosen is truly worth the sacrifices."

"Only you can answer that," Charlie said quietly, giving her shoulder a gentle squeeze. "But whatever you decide, I'll be here to support you."

"Thanks, Charlie," she whispered, a ghost of a smile gracing her lips. "I appreciate that more than you know."

As Sarah turned away from the pier, the last glimmers of daylight fading into twilight, a sense of finality settled over her like a shroud. The path she had chosen had forever changed her, and now she was left to question if it was truly worth it.

"Come on, Sarah," Charlie said, falling into step beside her. "Let's go home."

"Home," she echoed, a bittersweet taste lingering on her tongue. "That sounds... nice."

"Then let's make it so," he replied, his voice steady and unwavering. And as they walked away from the edge of the world, Sarah knew deep down that nothing would ever be the same again.